"Kiss me, Lakota. Not like before. Like you really mean it."

Her exhale brushed his lips and she shook her head again. "I can't."

"Why?" he asked, lacing his fingers with hers, bringing her closer.

"Because you want to kiss me."

A full smile bloomed. Holding her, he guided her head to his chest, bowed his head and kissed her cheek. Her eyes sprang open and she blinked several times.

Rob wasn't sure what she was going to say or do, but he didn't move and neither did she. She was in need of care, in need of love, and he had so much to give. He knew she did too. He just felt it. Nestling her in his arms, he softly bathed her cheek in kisses.

A fraction at a time, she moved and he finally kissed her nose. She shook a little, as if a slice of thunder rippled through her body, but she didn't back away. She pressed her shoulders a little closer into him, her face angling up just a little more, her eyes open, looking at him.

He touched his lips to hers. Then looked at her again. Her hands were on his arms and he felt her fingers graze his cheek. It was too soon to take her to bed, but he wanted to show her how a real man loved a real woman. Her lips parted and their tongues met.

Books by Carmen Green

Kimani Romance

This Time for Good
The Perfect Solitaire
Sensual Winds
The Perfect Seduction

CARMEN GREEN

was born in Buffalo, NY, and had plans to study law before becoming a published author. While raising her three children, she wrote her first book on legal pads and transcribed it onto a computer on weekends before selling it in 1993. Since that time she has sold more than thirty novels and novellas, and is proud that in 2001 one of her books was made into a TV movie, *Commitments,* in which she had a cameo role.

In addition to writing full-time, Carmen is now a mom of four and lives in the Southeast. You can contact Carmen at www.carmengreen.blogspot.com or carmengreen1201@yahoo.com.

THE PERFECT
Seduction
CARMEN GREEN

KIMANI™
ROMANCE

To the Sparrow:
I feel your love every day.
I love you.

 KIMANI PRESS™

ISBN-13: 978-0-373-86145-3

THE PERFECT SEDUCTION

Recycling programs
for this product may
not exist in your area.

www.kimanipress.com

Printed in U.S.A.

Dear Reader,

I hope you're enjoying reading about the Hoods. They are an amazing family that I've been able to create with your blessings. It's always fun to step outside the norm and write about something I truly believe in, but it's another thing for people to embrace that work and make it successful. You've done that for me and I appreciate your generosity.

Please write and let me know your thoughts on the Hoods or any of my other work. Visit my blog at www.carmengreen.blogspot.com or e-mail me at carmengreen1201@yahoo.com.

Continued blessings,

Carmen

Chapter 1

Jolted from a heavy sleep by frantic gloved hands, Loren Smith struck back at her attacker, hoping that her life would be spared.

She tried to scream, but could only cough as intense heat seared her lungs. Two firemen came into focus, and Loren realized this wasn't an attack but a rescue.

"Your apartment is on fire and we've got to get out of here," one said firmly.

Loren stabbed her feet into her running shoes and grabbed her large emergency duffel bag that was always packed.

"We're going out that way," the fireman said, moving her swiftly toward the window.

"I can't," she screamed, shaking. "I'll die."

She could hear crackling and bursting beyond her bedroom door and she knew there was only one choice. But she froze in place and didn't reach for the fireman who'd stepped onto the ladder outside the window.

Instead she saw her ex-boyfriend of two years ago, Odesi, who'd stabbed her and then tried to throw her out the window as if she were waste.

Loren pushed back with both feet. The fireman behind her took the bag from her shoulder and tossed it out the second-story window. He grabbed her around the waist and lifted her off her feet. "What's your name?"

"Loren. Loren Smith."

"Loren, I'm Lieutenant Tim Heath. I will not let you die," he said quickly and forcefully. "You will be safe. Lieutenant Tuggle will assist you down the ladder. Do not look down. Now, go!" Loren closed her eyes, and just like that the nightmare returned.

Odesi stabbed her... The paramedics arrived in time... The doctors saved her life... You will never model again.

Tuggle jostled her as embers of her life sprinkled down around her. "Stay with me, Loren."

Finally they were on the ground.

At the bottom she was placed inside the ambulance and given oxygen. The TV camera lights beaming into the small windows. There was pandemonium and all Loren could register as a mask was shoved over her face was that her safe haven of two years was being devoured by flames.

Chapter 2

It was still black out, but dawn would approach in hours. Rob Hood tried to hide his gun when he realized the sobbing intruder was Zoe's friend, Loren, but she'd already seen it. He held up his empty left hand.

"Please, don't shoot," they both said at the same time, he with the gun, she with defense spray.

"I won't shoot you," he said, putting the gun on top of the baker's rack. "Why are you here? Why are you crying?"

"Why are *you* here?" Her back was against the quartz-stone kitchen counter, and she was braced to run. This was more than deer-in-the-headlights want to run. Real fear filled the distance between them, and he knew she would have fought if anything got in her way. Rob held up his hands to let her know he wouldn't stop her or hurt her, and even in her mania he hoped she recognized his desire to keep things calm.

Gripping his crutches, he maneuvered slowly, careful not to put any pressure on his new knee. "Loren, what's wrong?"

"I called Zoe not more than five minutes ago, and she didn't mention that you were here in her house. Never mind. I'll leave." Loren's accent enthralled him; the weighty resonance of it made him want to close his eyes and listen to her as one would a smooth jazz piece. He knew of her African American/Native American heritage because he'd heard Zoe mention her best friend's ancestry. He'd been house-sitting at Zoe's suburban Atlanta house for a week while his twin brother, Ben, and Zoe took a much-needed vacation. The house had been empty—until now.

Loren kept her right arm braced against the center of her body, her hand balled into a fist.

The exotic woman, even without makeup, was beautiful, with smoldering green eyes and cheekbones that were high over expressive full lips. She looked scared. He knew from Zoe that the former hugely successful runway model had been disfigured by a boyfriend. That she'd become a virtual recluse.

"Zoe owes me an explanation," Loren said, wiping her eyes.

Rob recalled meeting Loren the past summer at his house. His attraction to the fair-skinned woman had been immediate, but his curiosity over her desire to be alone had catapulted her into his thoughts repeatedly over the months.

Though he'd mentioned helping the troubled woman through her difficulties to Ben and Zoe, they'd relayed her refusal. The fact that she was before him now was like a dream come true and a nightmare rolled into one. Loren wasn't at all happy to see him.

"Zoe and Ben went on vacation because they wanted to spend some quality time alone. I'm sure you know how much they love each other. Besides, ever since we solved the robberies in her stores, Zoe's been going nonstop. They both needed some downtime."

"Stop. I don't want to hear about my best friend from you. I don't believe a word you're saying. Zoe would have called me. She hasn't been gone from here in Atlanta that long."

The house phone rang and she watched as Rob picked it up. "Zoe, your friend is here and she's scared." Rob took his time getting to the table, his knee tender because he'd just run on it from the bedroom. "I'm putting you on speaker."

"Honey, please don't be alarmed—" Zoe pleaded with Loren over the air.

"Too late," Loren snapped, and eased over to the table as Rob pivoted on his crutches and walked back to the doorway that separated the kitchen from the dining room.

"I'm so sorry. Rob is there recovering from surgery and needed to be in a place that had a bedroom on the main level."

"How could you forget to tell me that you have a man staying here? I can't stay here. And he has a gun."

"I had my gun because I thought you were an intruder. You can stay here," Rob assured her.

"Butt out," Loren snapped at him.

"Loren," Zoe chided. "He's right, you *can* stay there. Rob is in the guest room downstairs and you can stay in my room upstairs," Zoe explained. "That way he won't have to navigate the steps."

"Why can't he go somewhere else? I thought you told me there were a lot of Hoods? He's got like two sisters and ten cousins and another brother, besides Ben, right? Why can't he go stay with one of them?"

"A slight exaggeration, but yes, sweetie. I'm sorry I didn't tell you he was in the house, but I was so caught up with the news of your apartment, I forgot. But there's more than enough rooms to choose from, and you both are mature adults. You can share living space. He's a good guy, sweetie." Zoe's voice was speaking in an empty kitchen. Loren had gotten up and walked back through the den to the foyer.

Rob hobbled on his crutches to the stairs and watched her get her things together.

"Loren! What are you doing?" Zoe demanded.

"Nothing, Zoe. We'll work it out." Loren had a gazelle-like stride that carried her back into the kitchen, where she grabbed a bottled water out of the stainless-steel refrigerator, and she straightened up the table until everything was exactly as it had been before she arrived. "Everything will be fine. I'll call you in a couple days."

"Promise me you'll stay."

The woman was nothing if not a whirlwind of determination. I can't promise, but I'll let you know if I go somewhere else." Loren sighed.

Rob had placed the phone on the table, and before he could get back, Loren had it in her hand and back onto the base. She eased past without touching him and was up the stairs in a flash.

"Where are you going?" Rob asked, hoping he wouldn't have to wrestle her for the room.

"To get a change of clothes, and then to a hotel."

When Rob got up the stairs, she'd already been through Zoe's closet, chosen what she wanted and was about to head past him when he stopped her.

"What are you doing up?"she demanded. "Zoe said you're staying in the bedroom downstairs."

"I was going to stay in there but the TV doesn't work. Besides, I'm all settled in this room."

Loren's look said she didn't think much of his answer. "You should go home."

"I don't have a car. And I'm comfortable here." He watched her closely. "You look like hell." Tall like most runway models, she was at least six foot, but tonight she looked small in her nondescript sneakers and borrowed sweatpants, her black hair frizzy and unkempt.

He'd heard stories of how her career had ended, but tonight he saw that she was truly only a shadow of her former self. "You've got bruises that are turning purple. They're going to be scary-looking tomorrow."

"I've had worse." Loren took the stairs down quickly.

"No hotel worker in their right mind would rent to you. You look like a woman that's got trouble following her."

Rob was at the top of the stairs and he could see that she'd finally stopped at the front door. He took his crutches in his right hand and hopped down a few stairs, holding on to the railing.

Her face was in profile, tear-streaked and stressed. When he'd been on the force, he'd talked criminals into turning themselves in, but he couldn't bet whether Loren would walk out the door.

"Your best friend wouldn't recommend you stay here if I were some type of crazed psychopath. You can leave, but you'd be hurting yourself worse."

Still, she reached for the doorknob.

"Loren," he chided. "Don't be so stubborn."

Her fingers slipped off the knob. Rob watched her for a few seconds. "The bed is made and the bathroom is clean. If you want to talk—"

"I don't want to talk about anything." The weight of the world looked as if it rested on her delicate shoulders. Her nose was red from crying and her wavy black hair was limp and in need of washing. She seriously needed to cry and then sleep.

"Okay. You don't have to, but I'm a good listener."

"Are you some kind of armchair psychologist? My life isn't Monday-morning football. I don't want to talk! I'm not your friend and I don't want to talk to you."

"Okay!" Rob almost laughed, but he could see that wouldn't go over well. Loren wasn't like one of his sisters, all of whom had thick skin and were used to his teasing.

"Good night." He turned around and went into his room upstairs, closing the door behind him.

He lay on the bed, the lights off, and wondered what she was doing. Three distinctive beeps answered his question. She'd set the alarm and left.

Rob turned over, closing his eyes. DeLinda, his wife, appeared, and he knew it was because she and Loren favored so closely. But DeLinda had been dead for two-and-a-half years now, and he only saw her in his mind's eye. He could no longer feel or smell her. She was gone and his heart was ready to love again, but he hadn't met anyone.

He'd thought he'd been right about Loren, but apparently not. Sleep crept over him.

He could hear the lower master bathroom shower started and his eyes slid open.

Rob closed his eyes and saw Loren and the challenge she presented. He took a deep breath and let it seep out of him slowly. He'd never met a challenge he hadn't won over. He'd start by feeding her.

He made his way downstairs and started breakfast just as the sun yawned its awakening.

Chapter 3

Loren felt feral in her anger for Rob Hood. He's probably just like all men: not able to be trusted. Why couldn't he have just left?

He was making it impossible for her to rest. Impossible for her to think or to move on with the next phase of reclaiming her life.

She lay on the bed in Zoe's pajamas, which looked more like capri pants on her long legs, and stared at the locked bedroom door with the chair wedged under it.

Her eyes grew heavy with sleep, and the papers she'd been writing on crinkled under her weight. Rob Hood was not trying to break into her room as her mind wanted to imagine, but he was singing and doing a terrible job at it.

Getting up, she took the hoodie off the chair and zipped it to her throat. Opening the locked door, she was stopped at the aromatic pleasure.

What in the hell did he think he was doing? The kitchen was her domain. Loren knew the thought was irrational. Rob probably didn't remember she was a caterer. She'd only been to his house one time, and that was when Zoe had asked her to cook for them.

Now Zoe was in love with Ben and off gallivanting on some island.

Walking through the dining room to the kitchen, Loren found a plate of food on the counter with a note.

On the deck watching the sunrise. Join me.

He'd made eggs over easy and hot dogs. Her most favorite breakfast in the world.

Her gaze ricocheted to the phone. The only way he could have known that was to find out from Zoe.

Her tongue slid across her teeth and her mouth watered. She thought of her freezer full of Sahlen's hot dogs from Buffalo, New York, that were all ruined now. And here she had one hot dog, no bun, a dollop of ketchup on the side. An all-protein breakfast, just the way she liked.

She picked up the plate and considered her options. She could go outside and eat her food with him and watch the sunrise. Or not.

Suspicion doused the tiny bit of comfort she took in his thoughtfulness. What did he want in exchange for making her breakfast? Sure, he was being nice now, but all men were nice at first.

The day would come when Rob would likely turn into an angry, violent beast, and she'd think back to today and wonder why she'd ever walked outside.

Taking her plate into the dining room, she sat at the table and dipped her dog into the ketchup before biting. There wasn't a better hot dog on the planet. Her back to the sunrise, she saw the beautiful fireball crest the horizon in the framed print of van Gogh's *Sunflowers*. She wished she'd actually gone outside to see the real thing.

All the work that had to be done to restore her life crowded in her mind, and the perfect eggs she'd been enjoying turned flat when she glanced over her shoulder and saw Rob outside, looking at her, one crutch under his arm.

Rising quickly, she went into the kitchen and tossed the rest of the food in the trash just as he pushed open the patio door and hopped in.

Loren braced her hands on her hips. "Just so you know, you don't have to feed me."

"Is that a Loren Smith thank-you? Because it needs improvement."

He threw down the *Financial Times* and she noticed the stocks he'd circled and had put exclamation points next to. Apparently he was doing quite well in the unstable market.

She'd expected sympathy, not abrasiveness. "I was getting to that. It was a nice gesture, but…don't do it again." His eyes widened and he smiled as if she'd told him all of his stocks had tripled and split. "I want to be alone. Doesn't anyone get that?"

"Not a lot of women shock me, but you're like the lottery ticket I played only once and won." He shrugged. "I'm glad I don't have to dance around your feelings. You know you're gorgeous, but not so nice." He winked at her. "Let's just leave it at that."

He hobbled over to the table and sat down, propping his leg up on the chair beside him. Wearing blue-striped pajama pants and a faded blue T-shirt, he was completely comfortable with his bulging muscles and his curly black hair.

She'd always had a soft spot for dark men with full lips and natural hair. In the modeling industry, a lot of men put chemicals in their hair to make it straight or curly, but Rob's was natural and short. She liked it and didn't want to.

She looked away. As it was unseasonably cool for September, he hadn't been wearing a robe while outside, but he reached for it now, trying to grab it with the tips of his fingers. His injured leg edged toward the table and his pain was imminent. She couldn't let him hurt himself.

Loren lifted the robe with two fingers and handed it to him. "Thank you."

Instead of feeling better, she felt worse. Before she swallowed the words, she let them come out of her mouth. "You're welcome."

"See, not so bad."

He didn't know. It was bad. He was too close for comfort.

He sat there, staring up into her eyes as if he was Nick Ashford and she was Valerie Simpson, and they were on the Reunited poster or something. Her mother and father had worn that song out dancing to it when she was a child. She turned around to leave the kitchen and got as far as the door.

"Hey."

The sharply issued word made her turn back. "The name is Loren."

"If I cook, you clean up, and vice versa."

She put her hands on the door frame. "I didn't ask you to cook for me."

"But you ate, and in my book, that's consent. Second rule, no fighting."

"With whom?"

"Each other." He made the statement as if she should be completing all of his sentences.

"That's ridiculous. If you're trying a crafty way to shut me up, then forget it. I'm going to speak my mind, and if that results in an argument, there's a place that leaves the light on six point six miles away. If you start now you can hop all the way there."

He threw his head back and laughed. "I have squatter's rights. I was here first."

"You have no rights. My friend is being too nice to get rid of you. But she's been too nice in the past and she's learned from her mistakes—too late, of course. But you might want to start packing. When she wakes up, she'll be doing a clean sweep."

"Wow, bitter doesn't look good on you."

Loren crossed her arms. "Live my life and then tell me what looks good and what doesn't."

"What was your life like?"

She glared at him. "None of your business. Are all you Hoods alike? Nosy, getting into other people's business?"

Rob nodded, and she felt worse that her insults didn't work.

"Are you leaving?" she asked.

"No. You're stuck with me. By the way, your accent is very nice. Why do you have one if you were born here?"

"Not that it's any of your business, but I grew up speaking three languages. English, Italian and Lakota. My accent is a blend of all three. As I grow older, I realize how much I sound like my mother before she went deaf."

"It's beautiful."

The anger she'd felt dissipated. "When I pray, I'll be sure to thank her for you." Sighing, she straightened her hoodie. "And while we're at the rules portion of breakfast, no singing."

"Negative. I like to sing."

"You're terrible," she complained.

"You're mean, and I can only hope that will change," he shot back. "So singing is in."

"Don't cook for me."

"I was being nice, Loren."

"It's Lo-ren. Not Lauren."

She sounded almost Texan and he suppressed a desire to laugh aloud. "Okay, Lo-ren. I'm used to cooking for ten, so if I cook and there's something left, don't think it's for you, but if you take one bite, you have to clean up the dishes."

She glared at him. "Fine."

"Fine. Another thing—no men sleeping over."

She laughed. "No men? Not a problem. Only women work for me."

He raised his head. "I see, you're gay. That's disappointing, but you do you. Then no women for you, either."

She picked up the pot holders and threw them at him. "I'm. Not. Gay. You. Idiot."

Rob ducked as best he could, but the last three tagged him in the head and neck. "It's normal to seek pleasure—"

Loren picked up a lead crystal decanter of olive oil that Zoe kept on the counter. Though nearly empty, the vase was heavy enough to do damage. "What were you saying?" she asked.

"I wasn't saying anything." Rob smiled as if he was enjoying her immensely.

"I believe you were attempting to discuss my sex life?"

"If I were discussing sex, *Kama Sutra* lotus position is especially effective. The woman sits on her man's knees—"

Loren heard herself making bizarre choking noises. She yanked open the silverware drawer and began dropping spoons and forks all over the kitchen floor, followed by the contents of the olive oil bottle. When everything was empty, she let out a relieved breath.

"That's not nice." Rob chuckled, admiring her fighting spirit. So different from the sad woman who'd walked in last night. "You know I can't get around that mess on my crutches."

"Maybe one of your sex positions will help you slither out of here. *Do not* speak to me again."

She spun on her toes and pranced out.

Chapter 4

Rob had never known a woman to hibernate, but Loren had managed to stay secluded in her room for the past week, hardly coming out when he was around. So he revised his game plan. Instead of making foods that didn't require much preparation, he began to cook from scratch, hoping to lure her out of hiding.

As if on cue, spaghetti sauce bubbled and popped, and he didn't bother to clean it up. He was playing a risky poker game of Texas Hold 'em, and his hand was full of cards that didn't match. Increasing the flame on the noodles, he let them boil over, watching the starchy mixture seep into the crevices of the burner.

Loren would be furious, and he was counting on that. She was, by far, the most stubborn woman he'd ever met. She'd not uttered a word to him in seven days.

"Stop cooking. You're making a ridiculous mess."

Her husky voice startled him, and Rob turned around to face the freshly scrubbed woman. The five pounds she'd lost made her look slightly gaunt. "You've been eating a little, so the end justifies the means."

"No, it doesn't. I'm not cleaning up another one of your mega messes. I'll eat yogurt until Zoe gets back."

"That's no way to live when you can have homemade spaghetti and garlic bread."

Rod didn't wait for her consent. He dished her up a plate, set it on the table and turned his back as if he didn't care if she ate or not. He served himself and began to eat, standing up.

Loren hadn't taken a single bite, and he knew he was losing this hand, but he wanted to bluff a little longer. She reached for the refrigerator handle and he eased closer, pressing his advantage. She backed off.

"What do you need?" he asked.

"A strawberry yogurt and a spoon."

"Try the spaghetti," he said casually.

"No."

"Why not, Loren?"

"I'm not cleaning up the walls, the floor, the ceiling and the countertops. A plate of food just isn't worth it. Excuse me." She reached for the refrigerator again.

"Eat, Loren. It won't hurt you."

Her expression shut down. She pulled her lips into her mouth, and started out of the kitchen.

"What's your deal?" he demanded. "I can't be nice to you at all?"

"I would prefer it that way."

The soft reply stung. "What will happen if I keep cooking for you or being nice to you?"

She finally looked at him. "Absolutely nothing."

That cut deeper. "I've never met a more thankless woman in my life." Rob made the matter-of-fact point and turned off the boiling noodles. "I know you didn't ask me to do anything for you, but there is this thing called human kindness. It's that intangible thing that one human being offers another when they see a need."

Her cheeks reddened and a thousand protests seemed to rise within her. "I'm sorry. I simply don't need anything from you."

"That's the thing about kindness. It's given without a question of need or want." As he said the words, her apology was working through him. "I accept your apology, anyway. Will you eat?"

She shook her head. "But I will stand here while you eat."

Rob could see the effort it took for her to make the offer. She stood between the kitchen and the dining room, and he realized they'd made a breakthrough. "Would you like a fruit smoothie? I have strawberries, mango, pineapple and yogurt."

Her gaze darted around the kitchen. "No. I'm not cleaning up this mess, Rob."

He laughed and folded his poker hand. "Fair enough."

"I'll have a fruit smoothie," she said softly. "Over here."

He noticed how she used the arched doorway as her safety zone, and he decided he wouldn't push his good luck. Using his crutches, he went to the refrigerator and pulled out the fruit. "One smoothie coming up."

Loren waited until four in the morning to clean the house, then went back to bed, frustrated that a man on crutches had so smoothly worked his way into her thoughts. What was he really doing here in his brother's girlfriend's house? Was he hiding out from some crazed girlfriend? She considered the idea, but he didn't act as if he had a girlfriend.

She'd been there a week and he didn't get calls in the middle of the night. His BlackBerry wasn't blowing up all the time, and he didn't speak in a hushed tone and rush into the bathroom to take his calls. As a model she'd seen all aspects of how men played games with women, but Rob seemed to not be in that crowd of single men.

So why was he here? If he took the upstairs bedroom, why didn't he just go home? She dozed off, no closer to answers than she had been before going to bed.

It was nine o'clock in the morning, and Rob was sitting on the backyard deck, doing leg stretches. Dressed to exercise, Loren drew in a frustrated breath. She wanted to go outside, too. Not with him, she reasoned, as she eased the silk sheers back in her bedroom for a better view of his strong legs. She *needed* to exercise. She was accustomed to running daily on her treadmill, but that had probably been destroyed in the fire.

She'd dreamed of Italy in the morning's early hours, and her father's house. There was peace in his villa, but she'd successfully hidden from Odesi here in the States, and she didn't want to give up everything and start running again. He'd vowed to come after her once he'd learned she'd survived his attempt to kill her, but he'd failed, and it was her intention to make sure he never succeeded.

Resting her unsettling thoughts, she settled her gaze on the beautiful line Rob's leg made each time he extended it. Scar and all, his knee seemed to be healing well. She didn't want to admit it, but since she'd been in Zoe's house with him, she felt a sense of peace she'd not known since childhood when she'd lived with her parents.

Her phone rang and she snatched it up. "Zoe? What took you so long to call me back?"

"Honey, I'm in Niagara Falls with Ben. Our Atlanta home is a long way from here. We've never been here before, and I thought we'd come up here for a couple days."

"You sound so happy."

"Loren," Zoe cut in. "Are you okay?"

"Yes, darling. I'm fine."

"You're not," Zoe said, her voice soothing in Loren's ear. "What's the matter?"

"Rob. He keeps doing things. He's everywhere. He leaves notes on the table for me to eat and take vitamins. Why is he so nosy?"

Zoe laughed until Loren felt foolish. She couldn't help the smile that finally broke through her sour mood.

"Do you hear yourself? He's cooking for you and you're unhappy. He's leaving vitamins and you're finding fault with him. Okay," Zoe said, reining in her laughter. "Maybe he's crossing the 'help' line, but your Do Not Disturb sign is made of kryptonite."

Even on his crutches, Rob patrolled the house as if he was some kind of cop. He checked all the doors and windows with a methodical precision she'd come to take a large measure of comfort in because she didn't have to do it.

She glanced out the window. Rob ran his hand from his knee to the top of his thigh and his muscle flexed. Her eyebrows moved up.

Even though he was trying to break down her walls, she couldn't help but admit he was succeeding on a minor level. And he was gorgeous. "I do wish he'd leave, though."

"Honey, if I were you, I'd get to know that man. His brother is a thoughtful, generous, intelligent man any woman would be proud to have as her own. He's all mine, too. And Rob and Ben share DNA." Zoe laughed.

"It's too hard to be angry with you. You're so happy. So go be happy with your man and I'll talk to you later. I love you, Zoe."

"I love you, too, Loren. Be nice to Rob. He's a good guy."

Loren rolled her eyes and hung up. Zoe's head was in the clouds.

Rob ran his hand from his knee to the top of his thigh and his muscle flexed. Her eyebrows moved up again.

He had a really big gun.

Touching her abdomen, she let the curtains fall. The scars reminded her of who she was and how unattractive she'd become. No man would ever know her well enough to see her scars. She just couldn't risk getting hurt again. But if Odesi's last declaration to see her in her grave was true, then she might need Rob's services. She shuddered and rejected the thought.

He could get hurt. Then Zoe would be hurt. The ripple effect would be too great. She'd have to go it alone like always and she'd be fine.

Rob's laughter curled out of him and tickled her. She eased the curtain back and watched Rob sign while he talked to his niece on the computer over a live camera chat. "You are a peanut head, darling. And you have to learn your spelling words."

Loren found herself smiling. She didn't know he knew sign language. She'd learned the skill after her mother had suffered hearing loss when Loren was eight years old.

Rob continued. "Don't Uncle Rob me, it's important, because peanut *is* spelled with an *A*. I'm not spelling it wrong, little girl." He laughed again, signing. "You don't hate fourth grade. You are the smartest fourth-grader I know. Yes, you are," he said, nodding. "What other words are on your list?"

Loren knew she was invading their privacy but couldn't look away.

"Sophistication, carnival, leotard, flippant. Okay," he signed, adjusting the computer monitor so he could see his niece clearly. "The flippant carnival worker lacked sophistication in his pink leotard."

His niece must have laughed because Rob threw up his hands, smiling. "What? That was a perfectly good sentence that was full of sophistication."

Loren laughed and Rob looked directly at her as if he could hear her through the closed window. Caught, she had no choice but to shake her head at him. He waved her out and she hesitated. He patted the space right beside him, and before she changed her mind, Loren backed away from the window and left the bedroom.

Outside for the first time in a week, Loren basked in the

Wednesday afternoon sunshine. Her hair danced around her face and she shook it back, liking the way the sun felt against her face. Rob's expectant look greeted her and he waved her over.

"Come on." He was so excited, she could hardly say no as she slid onto the picnic table bench next to him. "This is my niece Kacy, and she's been in trouble at school for not learning her spelling words. I've been helping her with her homework. Kacy, this is my friend, Loren."

His niece didn't smile or say a word.

Loren looked at the tiny camera on top of the computer, waved and signed. "Hi, Kacy, I'm Loren. I thought of a better sentence for your spelling words."

A gap-toothed smile began. "What is it?"

"Being flippant didn't work, so Uncle Rob had to wear his yellow leotard to Kacy's school to show his sophistication at the carnival."

Kacy popped up and down in her chair, shaking her hands in the air as the sign for clapping. "Uncle Rob, can I use that one?"

He frowned and shook his head. "That was a *terrible* sentence." He pretended to spit. "Nasty. Awful."

The ladies waved their hands again as they laughed at him.

"I'm using it," Kacy signed, a huge smile on her face.

"Think of your own, cheater pants," he signed, laughing at her glee.

Loren and Rob watched her write the sentence on the paper, and then Kacy tipped her head to the side. "Loren, you're pretty. Like a bird."

Loren laughed aloud. "Thank you, darling. I'll let you get back to your homework. It was nice meeting you."

"Wait," Rob said. He looked at Kacy. "I'm not pretty? I've been helping you with homework and nothing for me?"

Kacy grinned. "Uncle Rob, I love you googleplex, to infinity and beyond."

He signed, I love you, too. "All right, peanut. Can you do the rest of your work without me?"

"I guess so," she said, the webcam making Loren feel as if Kacy was with them.

"You know so, brilliant girl."

Kacy blew him kisses and Rob blew some back at her. His easy affection with the young girl was admirable. Feelings of longing swept Loren. She felt caught up in a storm of need and hope and pain. She tried to stand up but bumped the table, and though Rob didn't touch her, he put his hand out to stop her from leaving.

"Will you call me later so we can watch the basketball game together?" Kacy asked him. "You know Mommy hates basketball."

He gave her the thumbs-up. "I'll see you at tip-off. Love you, peanut."

"Love you, Uncle. Bye, Loren."

Loren waved, watching his niece, who looked so happy in her purple-and-pink bedroom. The longing had eased, leaving the pain she'd become familiar with. She settled on the bench, her hair flying behind her. "She looks like the happiest girl in the world. Was she born deaf?"

"No, she could hear until two years ago. She got very sick and caught a terrible virus. She was deaf within days. It about broke my heart. She loves basketball, so we watch TV and webcam each other, or when I can go to the games, I take her."

"Her father doesn't like sports?"

"He doesn't have anything to do with the girls now that he divorced my sister Mel."

"That's horrifying."

"She's a real trouper taking care of them all by herself. We pick up the slack when necessary so they don't want for anything. Mel wanted me to stay with her after the surgery, but I didn't want to add to her burden."

Guilt swept Loren for suggesting that he stay with family now that he'd explained his sister's circumstances.

"Zoe told me you and Ben are investigators. Can't you find their father and make him do the right thing?"

Rob considered her through hooded lids. "If we're taking care of them, what do we need him for?" His eyes had taken on a hard glint and she realized how important family was to him.

"I guess you don't. But do you feel that way because you're afraid he'll take her away from you?"

"First, I don't fear anyone except God. Second, a man that walks out on his family isn't a man at all, and he doesn't need for me to make him do the right thing. Hoods take care of their own."

Loren knew it wasn't his intention, but she suddenly felt like an outsider. She knew she wasn't part of the inner sanctum of Hoods, but being in this house with Rob had made her feel safe. She'd slept peacefully for two nights and that hadn't happened in years.

Rob was looking at her and she felt as if he was reading her thoughts.

She blinked to block him out and planned her exit.

"Loren, do you remember coming to my house last year? We were investigating the break-ins at Zoe's store and she asked you to bring food. My younger brother, Zachary, got on your nerves."

"I remember," she said softly. "The thief turned out to be the mall owner. He shot your brother. Is Ben completely healed?"

"Healed enough to go gallivanting across the globe with your best friend."

Loren hadn't minded helping out Zoe, who'd been a *best* friend when she'd needed one after she'd been injured. The physical injuries were healed, but emotionally she'd been a wreck from having lost her lucrative modeling career, and her mother. But Zoe hadn't prepared her for the Hoods. A family of men who could stop the breath from moving in her body.

Loren sat next to Rob, who, if given the chance, seemed like he'd put his arm around her. She moved away.

"I'd like to help you," Rob offered.

She pointed to his fresh scar and the crutches that were leaning against the table. "How are you going to help me? My home burned down. I have to find a new place to live and that's all. What can you do about that?"

"I suppose then all of your troubles will be solved."

She nodded, spotting a ladybug as it landed on a leaf. "Yes."

"Do you mind if I tell you something?"

Loren regarded him cautiously. "What?" Her heart hammered.

"Zoe said you were concerned about an old boyfriend named Odesi. Is he no longer a concern?"

Loren pulled in several deep breaths. "She had no right to tell you something so personal."

"Loren, what happened between you and him was all over the news. Just not the version Zoe told me." He hesitated, but she didn't fill in the blanks. "Let me tell you a little bit about my company, Hood Investigations, Inc.," Rob continued. "We solve problems. If it's finding a person, we locate him. If necessary, we neutralize threats and we protect at all times. We make sure that our clients receive the swift, fair justice they deserve."

Everything he said sank in, but she couldn't expose her fear to this fearless man. He was disabled, and though she felt better knowing he was there in the house with her, she would leave

Zoe's house as she arrived—alone. "Thanks, but you can't help me. I think I'll go inside now."

Loren hurried away and called Zoe once she was safely out of earshot. "Please don't tell Rob anything else about me."

"What happened now, honey?"

"Zoe, the more people that know about Odesi, the greater the chance that he will try to come after me again. I've managed to hide from him for two years, but that hasn't stopped him from trying to kill the one person he couldn't control. He's already tried twice since he attacked me in Monaco."

"What!" Shock echoed over the phone line and into Loren's ear. "When, Loren?"

"Last year was the tenth anniversary of my father's passing, so I'd gone to visit his grave site in Italy. Odesi must have known I would go, because when I returned to my hotel, he was there. We got into a heated argument and he began to choke me. Luckily the police were there and apprehended him. I left the country immediately."

"Was he prosecuted?"

"He was, but his father got him off somehow. Then I went to California to see a doctor about these scars and Odesi was in the parking lot. I have no idea how he found out, but I ran as far and fast as I could. I got back here to Atlanta and changed my numbers, e-mail, everything."

"Loren, why didn't you tell me?"

"You had your own problems, Zoe. Your sister was giving you a hard time. You were just divorced, and stressed about opening new stores. It wouldn't have been fair to heap more onto you."

A strangled laugh filled Loren's ear. "We're best friends, Loren! That's what friends do. They bother each other. They share secrets." Zoe sounded exasperated, but not angry. "Girl, I don't know what I'm going to do with you."

Tears rushed to Loren's eyes. "Keep me."

"Of course I will, silly woman." Zoe chuckled and sighed. "The Hoods can help."

"No!"

"Loren, that stubborn will may have saved your life once before, but it's not doing you any favors now. I'm not going to say a word to Ben or Rob for now. But remember this. When help is just a few steps away, you'd be a fool not to accept its offered hand."

"I can make it on my own, Zoe."

"Odesi has already come after you. Sick men like him don't stop until the job is done."

Chapter 5

Repositioning his knee for the eightieth time, Rob stared at the small DVD player on the bed as the surveillance video of the kidnapping of his deceased wife played. He looked for the one new clue that would crack the case, but today was like all the other days. At the top of the screen he saw a man who barely came into view.

"Gentlemen, have we done the countrywide face recognition on the man at the top of the screen?"

Speaking to Toledo, Ohio, detectives Ty Harrison and Stone Weaver, Rob was appreciative of their patience. They'd been trying to save his wife's case from being turned over to the cold-case department. There were only two detectives and two thousand cases in that unit because of budget cuts.

"We got no hits," Ty answered over the speaker on Rob's cell phone. The detectives were viewing the same footage, as was their customary practice. "But I try to sneak one in every couple days. With budget cuts, they want justification for each one."

On any other day Rob loved his job because he got to choose his cases. However, this one had chosen him. He wanted to solve it so he could put the memory of his deceased wife to rest.

"DeLinda Hood is dead, that's justification enough." Weaver was older than both Rob and Ty and his passion had kept the younger men going. Rob was glad he was still aboard.

"I appreciate that, Stone. I can't help but look at that clerk again. What's he up to now?" With both cops being in Toledo where the murder had taken place, it was easy for them to keep up on the suspects.

"He's a student at TSU, and his girlfriend just had a baby." Ben reviewed his notes. "That's quick. They'd just had one."

"S'nother girlfriend when you're a pimp," Stone supplied, his smoker's laugh filling up Rob's room by speakerphone.

"I checked on him last week through his probation officer. It was either school and work or going up for eighteen months." Ty filled in the blanks. "But what doesn't ring for me is why anti-nausea medicine? That's nothing to kidnap and rape over."

"Yeah, me, neither," Rob said.

Today marked the 1621st time he'd viewed the footage, but he was still missing something. "I feel like we're seeing the person but not looking at him."

The TV screen had been muted hours ago and he vacillated between the tape, the papers on his lap and the call. Who had killed DeLinda?

The file of pictures, handwritten and typed notes slid to the bed, and Rob leaned his head back and squeezed his eyes shut. He groaned aloud and the men on the phone made noises, too.

"I need a smoke. All these damned rules about smoking indoors and now outdoors. How is a man supposed to get any thinking done?" Weaver complained.

"I hear you," Rob said. "My knee is killing me. Hold on a second."

He needed to stop for the day and exercise his knee, and that included walking outside, but lately he hadn't felt like enjoying the September days, except to sit in the yard. He was too young to have had knee-replacement surgery. Maybe he was getting too old to chase bad guys.

During this second week of Loren being in the house, they'd become polite strangers, passing in the hallway occasionally, the kitchen their shared domicile. He would cook and she would clean, and that was the extent of their relationship. He wasn't sure how else to reach her, so he stuck to what he knew how to do. He cooked and she ate. He exercised and she watched from her bedroom window like a voyeur with a good hiding place.

He talked to Kacy daily, and Loren chatted with his niece, then ran back to her room immediately afterward.

"Can you take antinausea medication if you're pregnant?" Rob asked the detectives.

"No," Ty replied a half second off his usual quick time. "Where're you going with this, Rob?"

Suddenly the bedroom door rattled and he looked at it, but ignored Loren's banging. He switched off the DVD and turned on the news channel.

A photo of Loren flashed on the TV screen and her date of birth and death appeared beneath her photo. It was DeLinda dying all over again.

Shock prickled him, and a second later Loren hammered on the bedroom door again. She hadn't spoken to him since break-fast the day before. They'd become silent strangers who used the kitchen in shifts. He didn't go down there if she was anywhere in the vicinity. She'd said she needed her space and he obliged.

She banged on the door again.

"Come in," he said.

"Rob, I was thinking if a woman is—"

"Hold on, Ty. What is it, Loren?"

"I was trying to use my credit card to buy new cooking sup-plies, and they declined my order, saying they'd seen a report on the news that I was deceased! The lady on the phone accused me of trying to commit fraud."

Reflecting from her green eyes was fear and fury. In her voice, disbelief and anger. She held up the useless credit cards as proof and her hands shook helplessly. Suddenly she touched her forehead and her face crumpled, her fingers diving through her hair. "What the hell is happening to me? I've never done anything to anyone. I'm not dead. Loren Smith isn't dead. Why do they keep saying that?"

Rob pointed to the television. "Somehow the news got a mistaken report and ran with it. There's the shot of you in the ambulance. The reporters must have gotten you mixed up with the woman who was taken to the hospital." He pointed the remote and took the sound off Mute.

"The former runway model, well known for her exotic looks, later became famous for this impromptu dance number for fashion mogul D'Arby Knox. She succumbed to injuries sustained in a fire at her home. She was twenty-eight years old."

"I'm not dead. I'm not dead." Loren stared at him. "Rob, I need to work. They wouldn't let me use my cards. I called the bank and my accounts are frozen. The manager said he'd seen conflicting reports and I had to prove I'm alive. What am I going to do?"

"You just need to go down to the bank and show them you're not dead."

Even upset, with no makeup, her hair mussed, she was still beautiful. The bruises she'd sustained from being rescued from the fire had never fully developed and were gone like ashes.

"Uh, Rob, we can pick this up another time," Stone said in an even tone.

"No, fellas. Ms. Smith was just leaving."

Loren pushed her fingers through wavy black hair that covered her cheek. "I can't just go to the bank. Oh, my God. Somebody could steal all my money. I need it for—" The words drifted off as she went to stand in front of the TV and listen to the reports on her life and death.

He didn't question her. She had secrets. Namely, that she didn't want anyone to know she was here, that Zoe seemed to be her only friend, and that she didn't want to be nice to anyone.

"My business with the restaurants is going to be given to someone else. I won't have any work. Oh, God. What am I going to do?"

Her phone started ringing downstairs and she bolted, leaving the bedroom door open. Rob could hear her talking on the phone.

"Is that *the* Loren Smith?" Stone asked in a hushed, starstruck voice.

"Yes," Rob replied, using his crutch to swing the bedroom door closed.

"And you're not going to help her? What kind of fool are you?" Ty laughed.

"Days ago she said she wanted to be left alone, so I'm leaving her alone. But I didn't leave her alone at first. I helped her."

"Rob," Loren said from the crack in the door, looking mean. "Your brother wants to speak to you."

Chapter 6

Ty and Stone barely suppressed their chuckles. "Rob," Stone cut in. "I assure you that we'll keep working on DeLinda's file for the rest of today. We won't let it get sent over to cold case. You'll hear from us soon."

"Thanks, Detectives." Rob clicked the telephone speaker, ending the call, and turning the TV volume down.

He stared at Loren, whose mouth was turned down. He wanted to tell her about herself so badly, the feeling almost overwhelmed him, but he didn't. She was experiencing a crisis and she didn't know his pain. No one did. "Ben, what do you want?" he said into the phone.

"I heard you on the phone with the guys. How are you?" Ben's voice was full of love and compassion, and Rob's anger dissipated against his brother's sensitivity.

Rob watched Loren, who went into the hallway and sat down on the top step.

An image popped into his head of doing the same thing when Ben used to get into trouble. No matter what the punishment, he'd wait for his little brother.

"I feel like we're close to making a breakthrough. We're looking at the medicine."

"The antinausea angle. Who might have been pregnant, who might have just lost a baby. Maybe someone had cancer," Ben said gently. "Yeah, we went down that road. The guys didn't remind you?"

The memories all came back. The days, weeks and months after DeLinda's death. His frantic search and toss of the evidence. He hadn't left a stone unturned. He'd forgotten in the midst of his grief. "I guess they were going to remind me."

He caught Loren smoothing her hair behind her ear when she turned and looked at him. Her back curved. She needed him. Her eyes were still angry, yet pleading.

The knot was back, below his rib cage, above his stomach, and he hobbled back to his bed and sat down.

"I need a favor." Ben was talking again. Needing him to really listen.

"What is it?"

"I can't get back for a few days. Loren needs your help getting her life back on track. Conflicting reports have been made that she's deceased. When she called about a half hour ago, it was just her credit cards, but her bank accounts were frozen because someone went to the bank, claiming to be her and tried to withdraw money. The manager spotted the fraudulent ID, but as a precaution, Loren needs to go in and take care of this herself."

"Ben, she told me she didn't need my help. I've done as she's asked and left her alone."

"That was a week ago, and she was stressed out. Her apartment burned down, she's slightly agoraphobic, and scared of men. Wouldn't you have a bit of an attitude?"

Stunned, Rob looked at Loren again. She hadn't moved. "I might."

"Help her. Please."

Why was she scared to go beyond the seclusion of the backyard? Maybe she thought she was too old or that her looks had faded in the past two years. "What are you going to do for me?" Rob asked his brother.

"Not shoot you in your other knee."

"That's not funny. Had *someone* been there on time, I wouldn't have been chasing Madison by myself and torn up my knee."

"You still feeling sorry for yourself?"

"No."

"Come on, Rob. You could have stayed with Xan or Mel but you wanted to go it alone. That's not normal. Plus, our birthday is coming up. I know you're starting to feel helpless and sad that DeLinda is gone."

"It's more than that. I feel old. Maybe I should choose another career path."

Ben chuckled. "Man, we're Hoods until the day we die. We catch bad guys and teach them a lesson."

"That's the best part," Rob replied. "Just as long as we're helping people." His gaze came to rest on Loren's curved back.

"Of course. Hood justice is good justice. Now, help her."

"Zoe wants to speak to Loren," Ben said, relief in his voice.

"Loren," Rob intoned. "You're being summoned."

She got up and stuck her hand into the room for the phone. "Hello?" Loren half turned, talking into the receiver. "I am being nice. Yes, I am. Okay. I will be nic*er*." He could see her fingers on the doorjamb losing color. "I said I would, Zoe. No, I'm not crying. Bye."

Her fingers disappeared. He watched her shadow against the wall as she wiped her eyes on her sleeve.

Despite her sharp tongue and stalwart manner, his heart broke for her. "Loren, come in here."

She opened the door all the way and went to the end of the bed, facing him. "I'm sorry about disturbing your call, Rob. Months ago Zoe explained the circumstances of your wife's passing, and I overheard you on the phone just now. I realize you have more important things to do, like find your wife's killer. I'll try to be nicer to you."

Her apology cleared the air and erased any residual frustration he may have had. "I can see why being declared dead might be a little disturbing," he conceded.

He gathered up the grisly photos and put them back into the appropriate folders. There was only one that Loren looked at and that was of DeLinda. "She and I do favor. I'm just lighter than her. Do you know if she's Lakota Indian also?"

He shrugged, shaking his head. "I don't know."

"She is," she told him. "Sometimes you can tell a person's heritage by looking at their facial structure. Look at her mouth and eyes. She's part Dakota, too. She's American black by way of Somalia, Lakota-Dakota and maybe something else." She handed him the picture.

"How do you know?" Intrigued, Rob followed Loren's graceful finger as she leaned over a bit and pointed out DeLinda's facial features.

Her accent drew him to the Dakotas, a place he'd never been, and he wondered what she'd say next. "When you work with photographers and travel the world, you learn a lot about people from other nationalities. Our bone structure tells anthropologists about our ethnicity, the food we ate and the time in which we lived. Her bone structure and mine are similar. Our cheekbones are high and wide here, showing that we are Native Americans. Our mouth placement and lips, here—" she indicated on the photo and then her own "—also tell me she's of the Lakota-Dakota tribe. Now, our foreheads are slightly different. I am American black and Lakota, while she looks like she has stronger American Somalian genes. Our noses are also slightly different.

"DeLinda's body size is lean, as many Somalian women are, whereas Lakotas are more full-bodied. I grew tall, whereas my mother was short. My father was six four."

"That's very tall," he agreed, unable to take his eyes off her.

Her ears were small with gold hoops in them, and she studied the photo like an artist would another piece of art.

"Father was a scientist and we lived in Italy until I was eight, then I came here to live with my mother in the Dakotas with the other Lakota Indians. Perhaps your wife was part of a ritual killing, something that has nothing to do with medicine or being at a store at night or anything. You think nobody cares when a black woman is killed?"

He nodded. "I used to think that, yes."

"Be a Native American."

Her statement was like ice water in the face. Rob couldn't think of a reason why he hadn't considered this angle, but he'd never thought of his wife as Indian. She was black, but maybe not to others. "Excuse me for a minute." He dialed Stone and recounted their conversation, and halfway through Stone patched in Ty. They listened to everything he had to say and then ended the call.

The mood was now respectfully calm.

"Is there an easy way to let people know I'm alive?" Loren asked.

A reporter on TV emphatically stated Loren Smith was dead. They showed her in the ambulance with her head covered. It certainly looked as if she was dead, although she had only been disguising her identity. "I didn't want to be seen," she whispered.

Loren went to stand in front of the flat-screen TV, her worn jeans and T-shirt a perfect fit. She'd pulled off the hoodie and was holding it in her hands, the fabric bunched like an accordion.

Where she'd found clothes, he didn't know, but then he remembered the bag she'd come in with. There was a story with Loren. She hadn't left the room or gone farther than the back door. Her need for contact was apparent, but he didn't know when too much would be enough and she'd snap again.

"I'm not dead," she told the television. She turned to Rob. "I just want things back the way they were."

With all the papers and photos gathered and put away, a plan formed. "This could be a simple fix, Loren. Let's go to the bank and show them the obvious."

"Can't I just call them? I don't go out much anymore." She grabbed the sleeve of the shapeless jacket, pulled it on, zipping it. "I don't like going out. Maybe I can use my webcam." She paused. "I don't have a computer anymore." Her sigh was a half cry.

"That won't look real honest, anyway, Loren. They might think you're pulling a con."

"I'm alive, that's all that matters. Who confirmed that I was dead? They should have checked with fire lieutenants Heath and Tuggle."

"Unfortunately, we've had a record number of fires, there being a drought here in Atlanta, and the lieutenants were probably busy. Besides, their schedule is generally three days on and three off. So they may not have had access to the reporters or not have been sought for verification. Who knows? Not all reporters are diligent fact-checkers. Loren, it sounds odd, but I've seen this happen before."

"What am I going to do?"

"You're going to be okay." Rob found the role of comforter odd. The type of people he usually dealt with didn't generally seek his help, therefore their level of need for his advice was very low.

"I don't understand who would give false information and tell someone I'm dead. What do they stand to gain?"

"Nothing. This is a mistake. Let's just go have a conversation with a few people and get it straightened out."

He'd cleaned off the bed, but she sat in the chair instead, her face a mask of misery. "I don't want to leave. Can I give you a statement and you handle this for me? I just want to be left alone."

"Loren," he said gently, "maybe this is God's way of telling you it's time not to be left alone."

She gave him her mean look again.

"Ouch," he said.

"What?" She rubbed her forehead with the heel of her hand.

"Your mean look is hurting me."

She let her head fall back and then leveled him with a deadpan look. "Are you always such a girl?"

Rob chuckled, because he felt as if he'd taken a baby punch in the belly from his niece. "I think you need me. I *know* you need me. And you promised to be nicer."

She wasn't trying to be sexy when she drew her legs up into the chair. She was trying to hide her vulnerability, and he found that endearing. "I wouldn't be here if I didn't need your help. Can you—"

He waited.

Rob stood and took careful steps over to the wall that held all of Zoe's personal photos.

"How many Loren Smiths do you think have called today claiming to be you?" he interrupted. "We already know of one. According to these photos and the word from models in the industry, you were pretty well known."

She dismissed his observation of Zoe's wall of happy pictures. "That was a long time ago. I'm not that woman anymore."

He experienced a pang of regret and he clicked his teeth. "Damn. I really hoped to see that dance."

She rose. "You never will. That just won't happen."

"Well, one could hope. You looked so happy."

The room was quiet. He returned to the bed, where he sat down and began to write.

"I'm sorry," she said immediately. "I misinterpreted your words. I was once that happy person, but when you're young you don't know the type of danger that's lurking out there. I just don't dance anymore."

She paced the room, rubbing her forehead, staring at the TV. "When I wanted to die, I didn't. Now I'm here and they've killed me."

"When did you want to die, Loren?"

He couldn't imagine. When DeLinda had been killed, he'd known a loss he never wanted to feel again. But to wish himself dead had never entered his mind. What had happened in her life that had made a woman so vital want to be gone from the earth?

Loren's eyes sought his and he wouldn't let her look away. "Tell me," he said.

"Five months ago."

"Why?"

"None of your business."

"That's a defense mechanism to put me off. Tell me why."

"My mother died two years, five months ago. I wanted to be with her."

"Okay," he said as if he understood, but he didn't. There was a lonely place inside her he'd never known, and he'd been lonely.

"Why then?"

"It was my birthday and I'd awakened, expecting to hear her singing to me, and she wasn't there."

He understood loneliness and sadness. "I have two sisters, and when our mother passed, they took it harder than us boys. They all had so much in common."

"Yeah, you get it." Her voice held a note of wonder.

Rob nodded. "Loren, my plan will change your life. You're not going to be a borderline agoraphobic anymore. You're going to have to get back into public life if the world is going to believe you're still here."

"What do you have in mind?"

"Do an interview before a studio audience where you tell your story. That will get everybody out of the way at one time, and quash any rumors of death. You'll be telling the story in your own words, and news outlets can pick it up and replay it until everyone knows the truth."

She was already shaking her head and Rob could tell an explosion was seconds away.

"Why would you want to do the one thing I hate? No!"

"Loren, it's the best thing."

"What would DeLinda think of you all alone here in this house? You have a large family. Why aren't you letting them help you? I'm not the only one who's hiding, who's afraid. You're trying to shove me out there, and it's really you who's afraid of his own demons." She was already out the door, her fingertips all that was left in the room.

Rob was shell-shocked by her grenade toss. "Sit down," he commanded.

Loren reappeared in the doorway and came and sat on the bed.

"Don't ever do that again. You asked for my help and then threw it in my face. You don't have to like it, but you can say so and no problem. But don't attack my personal life because you don't like what's happening in yours. Now, you can do this my way or do it your way. Which is it?"

"I'm—"

"Don't apologize again. Just give me your answer."

She composed herself. "Your way."

"Now, excuse me so I can get dressed."

Chapter 7

Stunned by his hard tone, Loren looked contrite. "Rob, I'm terribly sorry. My behavior is deplorable. I'll not do that again. Of course I'll respect you and compensate you for your time."

"That's not the point. Ben asked me to do this and I said yes. The fact is that I respect you, and I expect the same in return."

"Of course. You're a professional and I shouldn't have insulted you. I—I… I'm sorry. Okay?" Her eyes hollow and dark from little sleep, she looked tired but sincere.

"Okay. Let's move on."

"Rob, to be honest, I'm no longer an outside person. I live a very quiet life, going out only when I have to."

He assessed her for a moment. She hid behind a blanket of hair. Clothes covered her body although the air was still warm outside. He was relieved to know she wasn't ashamed of her looks as he'd originally thought. She didn't cover her face except in high-stress moments, or hide her mouth when she talked. He was glad because her mouth was damned sexy. But she did cover every inch of her body. From her throat to her ankles.

"When do you have to go out?"

"Twice a week, when I make my deliveries. I bake desserts for two restaurants."

He hid his shock behind questions. "How do you get the supplies?"

"I order everything and have it delivered."

"Why are you like this?" Rob struggled to turn around and

watch her walk. There wasn't a lack of confidence in her stride, yet she moved as if she weren't in a hurry to get anywhere. "In all these photos you're outside enjoying yourself. All over the world. Don't you miss it?"

"Yes," she snapped. "But that was before my then boyfriend Odesi Tunaotu slashed me six times and tried to toss me off a balcony."

Rob swore, looking her over. "You don't look injured. Are you okay?" Those were the stupidest things he could say to a victim, he realized.

"I keep my body covered. I don't have a career because he disfigured me, so I have nothing to go outside for. I'm safer inside."

"But you weren't during the fire. Maybe that's why it's time to change. I'll help you, Loren, and I'll protect you." Rob jotted a few notes and then sent an e-mail.

She covered her face and he thought she might be crying. Rob moved toward her and reached out. His family was so physical, so loving. Her earlier question had driven a stake into his desire to be alone and nearly burst it. He *was* hiding, but he had reasons he needed to come to terms with.

His palm barely skimmed the tips of her hair. "No, please don't. I'll be fine," she said. She pulled the sleeves of the jacket over her hands and went back to the chair. "Do you need the kitchen? I need to think for a while."

He held his hands up. "No. I'm done, but be ready in about two hours. Is that enough time?"

"I'll make it enough. I don't want anyone to know where I live. Where I am. I don't want Odesi to find me."

Rob watched the TV again. A distraught man was being interviewed. "We had our differences, but the world will miss Loren. I always loved her," the man said, and began to cry for the cameras.

"That's Odesi. He did this to me."

Her throaty voice wasn't hysterical but matter-of-fact.

Incredulous, he moved a step toward her. "Why isn't he in jail?"

"The police in Monaco believed that I was into cutting myself as some models do. He lied to them and said he was trying to stop me and they let him go. Plus, Odesi's father got Odesi off the charges. Diplomatic immunity." She shook her head.

"The cuts were deep, I'm assuming?"

She nodded. "I was in intensive care for a week, and in the hospital a lot longer from all the injuries. They believed every word he said, and that I intentionally tried to hurt myself. Once they interviewed me and the surgeons who saved my life, they knew differently. By then Odesi was gone."

"Couldn't your tribe help you?"

Loren's laugh was bitter. "I couldn't go to my tribe. There is still tension between the U.S. and Native Americans because of unfulfilled promises. This is unimportant in the greater scheme of things. I've done things this way so he won't find me and finish what he started. I just want my culinary jobs back, and I want what's left in my apartment. I don't want people to steal the last memories I have of my mother and father. If they weren't destroyed by the fire."

This time her words reached inside him and that empty space didn't feel so hollow. Rob palmed his phone while handing her a pad and pen. "I have friends who can patrol your neighborhood. Then I can get some of my guys over there to move your things once the site is cleared. Give me your address."

"I'll pay them. You don't have to cover anything. I have money." She completed the address and put the paper on the bed, then backed away from him.

"Loren?"

She stopped at the door and she clenched her jaw, her hands

curling into fists. She faced him. Never had he seen such tension in a woman. He couldn't imagine how any one woman could be hurt so badly. He knew he would not, under any circumstances, touch her without her wanting him to.

But he couldn't stop appreciating her as any man would.

There was beauty in every one of her movements.

"No real man would ever put his hands on a woman except to love her. It's too bad your boyfriend didn't know how to love you."

Her eyes changed, and her mouth turned. "I will never let another man touch me. Ever."

Her words were like knives. Rob knew he couldn't atone for the sins of her former lover, but her hurt burned into him like acid.

"Loren, help works both ways. One day, you may have to help me. Just remember that. And another thing, don't ever associate me with the man who did those things to you. All men aren't alike. Step back from the door, I need to go downstairs."

Rob picked up his crutches and walked by her without a second glance.

Chapter 8

Exactly two hours later, Rob had just about everything in place. The interview was set at the national news station in Atlanta, and it would be broadcast right after lunch. He'd had to make serious promises in return because schedules were being changed, but a Loren Smith interview was a gem.

To have her appear live on the *City Limits* show was an absolute blockbuster! The industry would be abuzz with the news of Loren being alive, and his cousin, the producer on the Atlanta show, would be a real winner.

Rob was downstairs and Loren was sequestered in the room with all of Zoe's clothes, when the doorbell rang.

Rob stared at the door from his command post on the couch. He wasn't expecting anybody for another thirty minutes. Loren didn't really expect him to get the door, too?

"Loren, I'm not your servant and I don't work for you," he bellowed, his knee achy from therapy.

She walked down the stairs with a floor-length robe on, a towel around her neck, her hair in hot curlers. "Never said you were," she replied, her tone flat. Picking up the house phone, she pointed to a button from four feet away.

"This is for the intercom. Use it. Catch."

He caught the phone and she walked to the front door.

She stood behind it and reached around to give the man a fistful of money. He handed her a dress bag and she closed the door before he could see her.

"What was that about?" Rob asked, wondering what kind of illegal dealing he'd just witnessed.

"I just bought some clothes," she said plainly.

"From whom?"

"An exclusive store that makes home deliveries for the right price. There are two women lurking around the house."

"How do you know?"

Loren dashed up the stairs a full minute before his sisters broke into Zoe's house.

He had his gun drawn, but they had him covered, one coming in from the back and one from the front.

"Trap Team, that entry was terrible. I knew you were outside. If I were dangerous, you would be gone," he said to Xan, his sister who entered through the front door.

Xan, short for Alexandria was the oldest of his two sisters, and she gave Mel a disapproving look. "I told you we're getting rusty. This weekend, we're practicing."

"Fine. How are you?" Xan sat down while Mel walked around the house, familiarizing herself with the layout. She heard everything, but her style wasn't to be still. Her memory was picture perfect. She was at the mantel and then in the kitchen.

"I'm good. Knee is getting stronger every day."

Mel came in and sat down, too. "I just want to offer again for you to stay with me and the kids. We would love to celebrate your birthday with you, and you know how the girls love to cook for you."

Rob rubbed his sister's arm. He could tell by her eyes she still felt sorry for him. That meant she'd have the whole family over and everybody would stare at him all day and night, wondering when he'd find somebody else to love.

"The invitation is sweet, but I'm good here. I can think and get a lot of work done, but thanks," he told Mel, who was the best mother ever. "We don't have much time, so let's get to this.

Loren Smith, twenty-eight, was a victim of a house fire, and has agoraphobia. She's got an interview on *City Limits* at noon, but the situation is precarious. She was attacked two years ago in Monaco by a former boyfriend, Odesi Tunaotu, who is still in society. Loren wants to maintain distance from the public. She'll do the interview, then slip back into her quiet life. She doesn't like to be touched."

"*The* Loren Smith?" Xan asked.

"The one and only."

"Is she on any antianxiety meds?" Xan asked. The oldest of the Hoods, Xan was a full-time doctor, but as the leader of the Trap Team, she loved going out on assignment and taking bad guys down. Usually the Trap Team hunted straying husbands, but this assignment was unique and could use a woman's touch.

Rob shook his head, reviewing what he knew about Loren, which wasn't much. "That's a negative as far as I know. We need to double-check."

"Is she afraid Odesi will come after her again?" Mel asked, glancing up the stairs, her hair in cornrows, bound in a band at her neck. "Saw this whole thing on the news."

"Possibly, but the scars are emotional and physical. They ended her modeling career. I'm operating as base command, for obvious reasons, but you both are the eyes, ears and protection. This is a get-in-and-out situation."

"Is *City Limits* aware she's coming with armed security?" Xan asked.

"Yes, Tiki knows, and they know it's Hood."

"Rob, does anyone know she's here?" Mel asked from the window.

"Nobody knows anything."

"Okay, then why is there a man with a long-range lens looking at this house?" Mel clapped her hands once and they all looked, and she signed her last message. She was looking out the window from the lowest position on the floor that one could be and still see out the window. Compact in size, Mel held several black belts.

They all immediately switched to sign language. They'd all learned to sign when an ear infection had rendered Kacy hearing impaired years ago.

"Let's get Loren out of here. The interview is in an hour so we've got to jet. The connector has construction, so I've planned an alternate route," Rob told them.

Mel signed, "He's trying to figure out why he can't hear us anymore."

"What's going on?" Loren asked.

Loren had descended the stairs without any of them hearing her.

Rob watched his sister's reaction to Loren. Nobody said a word. They both had this look on their faces that said what his heart felt. Daaamn.

Loren signed. "Van or car?"

"Van," Mel signed. "You sign?"

"Yes, in Lakota and English. My mother was deaf for much of her life."

Rob stood up and took his crutches from Mel. "Okay, ladies. Xan, we'll hide Loren inside the van once you pull into the garage and lower the door."

"I'll make a show of taking your wheelchair out the front door. But you get in the van in the garage. No one will be the wiser when we drive away," Mel told them.

Loren signed, "You're coming, right?"

He looked at his sisters and they didn't move. He was the leader of Hood Investigations. What the client wanted, the client got.

"Yes, I'm coming."

"Then put some pants on," she said in that accent that made his stomach flip. "You're bringing down the whole family."

Rob wondered if Loren was actually joking with him, but she never smiled.

Mel signed, "I'll get them. Goodness, you're slow."

"Have a bag?" Xan asked Loren.

Loren motioned to her body. She had hidden it under the large Indian-print poncho she was wearing.

Rob handed each of them a headset and Loren backed away. "They will take care of me." She turned to Xan. "What are your signals for run, stop and go?"

Both of his sisters moved Loren away and showed her what to do if they needed her to follow them. Rob watched the strange dance and quickly dressed. Loren took the lesson seriously, catching on quickly.

Mel signed, "Rob said you have a touching issue. We will cover you if your life is in danger. Don't fight us."

Xan produced her business card and handed it to Loren. "Are you on any antianxiety medication?"

"No. I don't take any recreational drugs of any kind. I only take medication to sleep at night and natural herbs for phantom pain from stab wounds."

"Okay," Xan said. "If you're feeling anxious or start hyperventilating, we'll pull you out of there and get you over to Emory University Hospital Midtown on Peachtree Street within four minutes."

"Okay," Loren said in that throaty voice he'd grown accustomed to. She went back to signing. "I don't usually lose it. I just don't want to get hurt. What happens if he shows up?"

"We'll take him down," Mel said matter-of-factly.

"Loren, he was in New York earlier today. He doesn't know you're here. It would take a stroke of luck for him to find out you're alive *and* show up at the studio. Our concern is not only that you're safe, but that the other people around you are safe, too," Rob told her.

"Why would he come after you? It's been a while since the attack. Maybe he's moved on," Xan hypothesized.

"He came after me last year in Italy when I went to visit my father's grave site. I'm afraid," she said, and her voice caught. "I'm afraid if he knows I'm here, he will try again."

"You still haven't told us why," Mel said evenly.

"He believes I took papers that prove he preys on underage young women. It's not just that. It's all women. He used drugs to get them, and he filmed it."

Loren opened her palm and showed them the flash drive. She nearly closed her hand when Rob cupped her hand with his. He reached inside and gently took the memory stick.

"This has both video and print data?"

Loren nodded.

"I'm going to take good care of this and review it when we get back," he told her. "I'll give it back to you and you can decide what to do with the information."

"Okay."

"Well, then," Xan said, meeting her gaze. "We're going to make sure he doesn't get you. Ever."

Rob gave her a reassuring smile. "If you get scared, focus on me. Breathe in and out. Nothing is going to happen to you. Trap Team will be invisible unless you need them. But I'll always be where you can see me."

"Okay." A big breath shot out of her and then their gazes connected. "Rob, today I don't want to die. Don't let me down."

He felt as if he'd taken a punch to the diaphragm. "I won't. Let's move out."

Chapter 9

The lights were hot the way she remembered and the adrenaline rush was like an intravenous feed of Red Bull and cola. Standing behind the white screen, legs apart, cape disguising her body, cowboy hat low over her brow, Loren could have been anyone or no one. If she'd been fast enough she could have given the Hoods the slip and vanished, and no one would have known where to find her.

But she refused to have her life completely taken away. If she chose to live privately, that was one thing, but her former boyfriend wasn't going to steal any more of her joy. And a fire, an overzealous reporter and misfiled paperwork wasn't going to encroach upon her solitude.

She needed for the world to know she wasn't dead. She wanted to live now.

All she cared about now was her life. Her quiet life.

"Are you ready?" Tiki, the producer of *City Limits,* stood beside her with a headset on and a bottle of water in his hand in case she needed it.

Loren nodded. "I'm ready."

The signal was given to the announcer.

"This next guest will surely blow your socks off."

Loren uttered her line: "I'm back from the dead, darling." The music from her infamous dance cued. The white screen rose and she didn't do her anticipated catwalk. She glided toward the host, losing the cape first and, once she got to the stool, the hat. Loren fluffed her wild hair and the live audience erupted.

Their reaction was shocking, with applause that felt like a thousand hands running all over her. She tossed her hair back so it fell into place and gave her best smile. When they didn't stop clapping, she got up and bowed to each side, thanking them for the warm reception. She'd had no idea she'd been this missed. It was healing in some ways, but overwhelming, too.

A moment of panic set in and she looked to the right wing of the stage. Rob was there and she was able to take a big breath. She turned back to the audience and remembered every swipe of the cloths used by the nurses who had cared for her after the stabbing, and this touching was different. Both helped her. Bolstered her. She glanced again to her right and Rob was there applauding, too.

Gino, the host of the show, handed her a microphone to signal the beginning of the interview. The audience quieted.

"Heaven or hell? Where have you been for two years?"

"Baby, I've been to both. Heaven is better." Her voice was husky, the way it had always been, and she winked at the audience, which responded raucously.

"You're still so gorgeous! Doesn't she look great for a dead woman?"

Again, Loren was swept up in their wild applause.

Another glance at Rob, who winked and gave her the thumbs-up for a good answer.

"What are the rules of someone reporting your death and you're not dead?"

"Don't panic." She laughed and shrugged. "Don't run into the street, telling people 'It's me, it's me. I'm alive.'" The audience joined in laughing with her. "Well, if you want to be alive, dispel the myth. Act alive. A friend convinced me to come outside."

"Are you agoraphobic?"

It took her a minute and the applause was deafening. "Some. You know how you have an inside cat and an outside cat? I'm an inside cat."

Gino laughed, and his face settled into a very big grin. "Man, could I have fun with that, but unemployment doesn't look too good these days. What do inside cats do besides look out the window and wish they were outside?"

"That's what you think. They get outside and think 'These rats are as big as dogs, I'd better go home and eat the food out of the bowl my slave pours for me.'"

The audience went wild.

Loren laughed at her own words and slid back on the stool. She'd decided to stay a minute longer.

"Loren, what have you been doing?"

"A little of this and that," she teased.

"Come on," Gino pried. "You died a couple weeks ago, according to reports. So we need details. Where have you been? What have you been doing? We know your apartment burned down and we were all saddened to hear about that. How are you?"

"You're right. I'm doing okay. There are some really amazing firefighters who rescued me. Lieutenants Tim Heath and Lieutenant Tuggle. If it were not for them, I'd really be gone. So I thank God for their bravery and their patience. It's not easy getting someone with my long legs and problems out of a window and down a ladder. I was afraid and they were amazing."

The audience was generous with their praise. "For the past two years I've been in school getting a degree. I'm a licensed chef now, and I bake. Just for family and friends, and a couple restaurants in the Atlanta area. So while my life as a model is over, my real life as Loren Smith is just fine." She smiled and looked at Rob.

"You're a chef? Where can we taste your culinary delights?"

"Two small restaurants around town. I don't bake enough to feed everyone, so I can't give out the names of the restaurants."

"Oh, no." Gino waved his hand to garner audience support in his disappointment. "Well, I guess we'll have to understand because you're so beautiful. I have to ask, Loren, how do you feel about what people are saying about you?"

"I feel great."

"Even the unkind things?" he asked, with a hint of disbelief in his eyes.

"I will never worry about what people say about me, I can't do anything about it. I'm only responsible for what I say and do. I only welcome goodness into my life."

"Such wisdom from a woman so young. Now, you've still got the looks and the figure."

"I don't think designers will agree with you." She looked at the audience, which didn't agree with her at all. "I'm a size eight."

"I've got the world's smallest violin here for you sister, but," Gino said, "you're the role model young women need. Can you give us one sample catwalk, please? Audience, help me. Do we want Loren to do one of her famous catwalks, please?"

The crowd roared until she stood. "Just one, and I'm going to need some help. If I mess up, feel free to laugh."

The lighting guys gave her a spotlight and track music, and Loren began her walk, which was a sensual glide that was the complete opposite of the model strut. She made eye contact with the audience, connecting with them. When she reached her stool, she took her microphone and turned, accepting her accolades.

"Amazing." Gino grinned. "Once your life is back on track, will you come back and bake for us? We would love that, Loren."

She looked him in the eye and hesitated. "Sure. Yes, I will."

"Did you hear that? She said she'd come back!"

The audience went crazy.

Loren laughed as if she'd won something. "Now, can someone please turn my credit cards back on?"

Chapter 10

Rob watched Loren perform and she was a different person. This wasn't the same woman who didn't want him to touch her or even speak to him.

This was a sexy, tantalizing, exotic goddess. The sleeping lioness had awakened.

The next guest was late and Loren ended up staying on longer than scheduled. She wouldn't talk about the "accident" that ended her career, or her ex, but she did talk about her past and future in vague strokes that said very little. She wanted to own her own shop, a café or perhaps a location inside a department store.

She'd sworn off dating, telling the host that incidents in her past had soured her on relationships, but she was happy with the decisions she'd made.

Rob listened to Xan give updates about the growing crowd outside the studio exit. As soon as Loren was finished with the interview, they needed to move. He saw this getting bigger than Loren imagined, and he wondered if he had been a little too shortsighted in his view of how much the public had missed her.

"We've got company."

"Copy that. Who, Xan?" he said.

Xan was in the parking lot with the transportation team he'd hired to get them back to the house, while he, Mel and *City Limits* security escorted Loren back to the parking garage.

The interview was over and Loren was mingling. Rob was with her every step of the way.

"A man who says he was engaged to Loren."

Loren shook her head.

"Xan, she said she doesn't know him."

"Copy that," she said. "What's your ETA, Rob?"

"Our estimated time of arrival to the van is ten minutes. Everyone get into position. You didn't tell us you had crazy fans," he said to Loren. The volume of paparazzi that had gathered surprised him. They'd worked with CEOs and some minor celebrities, but never a model.

"You never asked." In the garage, Loren got in the van as photographers ran beside the vehicle. "Should you be driving?" Loren asked him.

"I got this. Look." He pointed to the note he'd written her.

Loren slid her hat onto her head. "Your sisters are driving the other vans. Why?"

"You'll see in a minute," he signed, and turned into a parking garage on Piedmont and drove up to the third level. Six trucks all different sizes were parked side by side. All the doors were open, and she was instructed to crawl through and told when to stop and stay down.

"I'll let you know when to get up," Rob told her.

"Where will you be?" she asked, sounding worried.

"Don't worry about me. You'll be safe. Be quiet," he told her, and covered her up. For a second his hand rested on her shoulder and she didn't feel even the slightest bit of panic. Before she could move, he was gone and the door was shut. The doors on all the trucks closed, one at a time.

As she lay there, the truck began to move, and she rested on a down pillow and blanket. Rob had thought of everything. This wasn't at all how she had planned to spend her day, but this wasn't the worst thing that had ever happened to her, either.

Rob had helped her get her life back, and the truth was she felt better than she had in months. The attention from his family had been nothing short of amazing. His sisters were loving people. They'd been so respectful of him. Having grown up without siblings, and entering modeling at a young age, she'd only seen dysfunctional family relationships. Stage mothers, crazy daughters. Drugs. Assault. Even death.

Nothing like the Hoods. Though she'd made it seem as if she wasn't paying attention, she'd listened to how his sisters had planned to get them both in and out of the station, and everything had gone flawlessly.

How would she repay Rob's generosity?

Her thoughts drifted. She'd told Zoe she would be nicer. The truth was, she could stand an entire attitude adjustment.

Her thoughts drifted and she dozed. The van stopped and the door opened.

"Wake up, Sleeping Beauty." Rob's hands again were on her shoulder and shaking her gently. Loren sat up, unfolded her legs.

Rob extended his hand. "You don't have to take it, but I figured you might be sore from being curled up for two hours."

Loren regarded the extended palm and touched it for a second as she slid out of the truck. He was strong and firm like the firefighters, and she didn't get the impression he wanted to hurt her. The revelation was surprising.

Easing her hand from his, she grabbed her hat and followed him into the house. "How did you beat me here?"

"I came by taxi. There's nothing more disappointing to a photographer than to see a hobbled man get out of a cab. You were brought by a floral delivery truck."

As soon as they entered the house, the truck backed out and the garage door was lowered. She exhaled her relief to be home again.

"People still think I'm dead?" she asked, amazed at the number of vases that filled the tables and overflowed onto the floor.

Zoe had been listed as her next of kin with Loren's modeling agencies. They must have directed all floral deliveries be made here. Some of the arrangements were elaborate, gorgeous. Loren walked to each one and gathered the cards.

"I guess they'd already been ordered."

They walked into the dining room and that table was covered, too. "It looks like a funeral parlor in here," she told him, circling, touching the petals. "How'd they get in?"

"My cousin Hugh was here. It's obvious you were well-thought-of."

"Can you not speak of me as if I'm not here?" She fingered the hat, still unaccustomed to the thought of being dead.

"Sorry, beautiful."

The largest white rose arrangement was from Odesi's father, a man she'd at one time been fond of, but who had a blind spot for his son.

"May I borrow your phone, Rob?"

Rob handed it over and she dialed from memory. "Ambassador, it's Loren. I am as well as can be expected. No, I don't need anything. Yes, I have accommodations. I agree, sir, your son is a fool." Her sad laugh was filled with heartache. "I will accept your blessings and ask you again to get help for your son. I will remain in hiding until he is no longer a threat to me. Good-bye."

She returned the phone and pulled the poncho over her head, and noticed Rob looking at the tail end of a jagged scar on her stomach.

He was quick, touching the chairs as he moved toward her. Pointing, never touching her, but close enough. "Is this what he did to you?"

His eyes reminded her of a panther. She flinched as if he'd hit her and he slid-hopped back a step. "I didn't touch you."

She snatched the shirt down. "The look on your face reached me first."

"It's fury, Loren. Nothing else. I have scars, too. Want to see them?" He took a step and his knee popped. Howling in pain, Rob hopped, reached for the table, a hand swipe too far to get to it.

Loren hurried and went up under his bent frame and caught him around the waist, her face coming even with his neck, her chest meeting his. His heart raced and he froze.

"Rob, it's okay. You're going to be okay. The couch?"

"Yes. Just get my crutches. They're in the kitchen."

"Why not get you settled on the sofa first? Just lean on me. I won't break." She looked up at him. His skin was so smooth. "Trust me. I won't let you fall. Lean on me."

For a man his size, she could feel the control he had of his body, but his vulnerability was in his weakest limb. He wasn't used to relying on anyone outside his immediate family. He was used to being the savior.

He was scared, she realized.

"My real name is Lakota Sky," she confessed softly. "Lakota Sky Thunderhawk. But I changed it to Loren after I met the great Sophia Loren as a child. She had lips like mine." She smiled at him and they took small steps toward the sofa.

His eyes were on her mouth and he was perspiring, but they were moving. "You think I don't know that you're trying to distract me?"

"I know that you know."

"You have gorgeous lips."

"Thanks, I can say the same for you."

"Why do you whisper?"

"Because we're standing so close there's no need to shout."

Rob was nothing but pure muscle. His chest filled the spaces where her breath left off. Just as she held him, he held her just as tightly.

"Does it hurt badly?"

"I'm not sure anymore. I've got a woman attached to my side and I can't think straight." He took a bigger step and grimaced. "Yes, it does. I have pain pills in the kitchen."

That admission cost him, she could tell as he tried to set her away from him.

"Don't do that. I'm not going anywhere." She held him tighter. "If you fall, I'm going down with you."

"Yeah?" he whispered.

"Yeah." His mouth was just inches away and she could have kissed him, but she didn't. She hadn't kissed a man in years. Hadn't even wanted to.

Getting him down onto the couch was the most important thing. She estimated another three feet and he could fall backward and still make it, but she wouldn't let that happen for anything in the world. "You did your job today, let me do mine."

"What's your job, Lakota?"

"Don't call me that."

"Why? You don't like your given name?"

"I love it, but people outside the community think I'm a novelty and want to exploit my looks for money. People inside the community want the same, but for political reasons, to further the causes of our people. I've never been politically ambitious. If you insist upon me reentering the world, I'll do it as Loren, not something as treasured as Lakota. We're here. Sit, carefully." She eased him onto the suede divan.

Rob sat down and pulled his leg up. He breathed slowly and closed his eyes.

"Lakota, only at home. Between us. Deal?"

She nodded. "You should take off your jeans so I can look at it."

It only took a second for both of them to start laughing. "I think you want me," he teased.

"In your dreams, Hood."

"In my dreams you *do* want me, Lakota."

Loren could feel her eyes widen and wanted to hit him. Instead she leaned a little closer. "If you felt better, I'd hurt you."

"I bet you would." He gingerly touched his knee. "I think it might be okay. I can move it, but I think it was just popping. The doctor said that would happen from time to time."

She moved her hair to one side, then the other. Rob's admiring looks made her feel like a woman, and she hadn't felt that way in a long time. "When I was recuperating, I learned a lot about muscles and what they're really capable of. You've been on this leg all day because of me." She looked at him, then away. "So, maybe I can repay you by doing some therapy that I learned. But the jeans really do have to go."

"I don't think you know me that well."

She grabbed an annoying gnat out of the air and let him go behind her. "You're not funny, Rob. I can call the doctor and tell him I heard the pop from five feet away."

"I think… No, I *know* you like me."

She wanted to smile, but pressed her lips together and moved her neck back so her hair fell down her back.

Loren sat back and met his gaze evenly. "I don't *not* like you. You did something extraordinary for me today and I should repay your kindness. We are sharing this home, and you are rather pathetic, so—"

"Was that a joke?"

"No."

"That was the second crack on me today." His eyes seemed to sink into her and search out her secret places of truth, and while he didn't use them against her, he did expose them to the light. "I think you want to be around me because...you can fill in the blanks here. Because you..."

She looked at him from the corner of her eyes. "I appreciate everything you did for me today. So I'll massage your knee. But don't think I'll start trusting you."

His face was so serious when she looked at him. "I won't ever think that, Lakota. Because after you just made me trust you, and after today, that would be terrible. Wouldn't it?"

Before she started crying, she moved away, wanting to hate him as she had yesterday and the day before, but unable to find the strength within herself to do so.

"I'm going to change clothes," she said. "Do you want some shorts or your house pants?"

"I'll get them." He pushed up on his knuckles as if he was really getting up.

"If you move, I'll call Xan and have her shoot you in the other leg. Do you want that?"

He smiled, and Loren could see why Zoe had fallen in love with his brother. Rob's mouth was the perfect shape for kissing.

She was staring, and he was, too, so she ran up the stairs and got him some shorts.

"Are you going to help me with these?" He put down the remote when she entered the room.

"Only if you're dead. I need to mix the oils. I think you can handle it."

She could hear him struggling, but she didn't stop as she walked through the dining room to her room to change her clothes. Removing her top and pants, she carefully returned them to the hangers in the closet. The satin and silk had felt so good today—the finery was something she'd not thought about in so long. She hadn't realized she missed being dressed up until now and was facing her sparse clothing options. She pulled on loose pants and a tank top.

Today had been good. Excellent, really. Today represented the best of what modeling had been about. There was a whole other side that she had disliked. The drugs, backstabbing and racism, among the worst. The savage scars crisscrossed her abdomen, chest and lower belly in caterpillar-like lumps. Some had flattened after numerous cortisone injections, but others had become keloid scars, and still looked angry. These itched like crazy and often had shooting pain. Those were the worst. She rubbed them before she dressed and went into the kitchen.

Confidence sinking, she reasoned, who'd want her? No man would want to touch these injuries and know that another man had done this to her. No man would want a wife he couldn't protect from the demons of her past.

That was why she was supposed to be alone. Odesi had seen fit to determine her fate. Now she was living out the result of his actions.

"Loren, I'm ready."

No matter any physical awakening she'd experienced today, she'd have to ignore those feelings because she was seriously damaged goods, and Rob deserved a healthy and healed woman.

But what would touching him do to her? Just being next to him had awakened a need in her to be close to a man. In these few weeks, she'd managed to stop crying. She'd laughed more today than she had in a whole year. At the studio, she'd held his hand. She remembered reaching for it several times and he'd been right by her side. He'd weathered her storms, her terrible tantrum the other day, and now she was going to give him a massage.

She felt like Sleeping Beauty, awakening from a deep slumber. Loren touched her smiling lips and forced them to stop.

"Lakota, I'm thirsty. Can I bother you for something to drink?"

She pulled a bottle of water from the refrigerator and put it on her forehead first. She and Rob Hood were sharing space and nothing more. "I'm on my way," she said, trying to infuse lightness into her voice. She made him a cup of tea and began to mix the oils.

Chapter 11

Loren tried to keep everything in perspective even when she heard the soothing strains of Dave Koz on the TV jazz station. She popped two heating pads into the microwave and snuck a glance around the corner at Rob, who was drinking water and relaxing.

He was resting his head on the back of the sofa, a grimace on his face, his brow dappled with perspiration. "Loren, can you bring me a pain pill off the kitchen table?"

He opened his eyes and she was looking right at him. "You're going to be okay, Robinson Hood. You are a protector of good. Try this tea first. It will relax you."

She picked up two bags. "For your back," she told him, and helped him lean up so she could place the first one on his lower back.

"Okay. What's in them?"

"They're heated peach pits from small peaches. You warm them up in the microwave or in the sun and put them on the painful part of your body. I gave these two bags to Zoe last year and she's never used them."

He picked up a smaller bag and shook it. "That's a lot of peaches."

"Yep," she replied, before kneeling on the floor and protecting the Ultrasuede sofa with leak pads and a towel. Loren then dipped her hands in the oil and began to massage the muscles around his knee.

"What's in that?"

"A few ingredients from the kitchen," she told him. "Just relax. In fact, you can lie down and let me go to work."

"No, I'd better sit up." Rob grabbed a pillow for his lap and watched her work on his quadriceps muscles. "How do you know this? Did you grow up on a—"

"What?" she asked, glancing at him, the hint of a smile on her lips. "Reservation? Everyone thinks that of Indians. We lived in a regular house like everyone else. I was born here, but lived in Italy with my father for eight years, then in the Dakotas with my mother. My mother was the first deaf female Native American doctor to graduate from Johns Hopkins. I learned about muscle therapy from the nurses and therapists at the hospital after my injury."

"That's amazing. How was Italy?"

"I loved Italy. My father was this very intelligent academic and he didn't believe life should have borders. When mother lost her hearing, I moved back to the States full-time to help her."

"Were they ever married?"

"Until they died, but they were volatile as a couple. Though there was much love between them, they could not live under one roof. My father objected to me being a model, and my mother believed in allowing me to follow my dreams. I have several degrees and many passions. They believed in education, but I only have one love."

"And that is—"

"Baking."

"What are your degrees in?"

"What are yours in?" she asked.

"I went to law school and I passed the bar last year. I decided recently if I can't chase bad guys, I want to be a judge."

Her eyebrows shot up and she didn't try to hide her surprise. "Well, that's interesting. I've never met a judge before."

"That's only if—"

She nodded. "I know. You can't run bad guys down and tackle them."

Rob grinned. "That's right. Now, back to you."

"I have a Ph.D in psychology."

Rob leaned back. "No way."

Loren nodded, her eyes cast down. "Yes, definitely. I graduated from high school at sixteen. I also have a bachelor's degree in Italian and psychology."

Impressed, he watched her fingers work on his knee, but he couldn't help but study her also. She exuded calmness now, when she'd been so agitated just a day ago. He liked this side of her and wanted to know more. "Aww. Now you're just showing off."

Loren giggled. "Sure, that's what I'm doing."

"Your father wanted you to follow in his footsteps." It was more a statement than a question.

She worked his muscle with her thumb all the way to his hip, and more than his quadriceps responded. The pillow hid his desire. Loren shrugged and nodded. "My father was very proud of his very smart daughter as was my mother. How do you feel, Rob?"

"Strange."

"How so?" she asked, frowning. "Your muscles are responding quite well."

"You perplex me. You told me to never touch you. Not to speak to you."

She didn't say a word for a full minute. "I meant it at the time, and I was being terribly unkind. I'm sorry."

"You were scared and stressed out. Then again, you don't live in the world alone and you seem to want to."

"I lived in my apartment alone, and I controlled how much I wanted to be involved in the world."

She went back to work on his knee. Gently she separated the muscles, and the tissue responded to her touch. Loren waved her hand over the scar, the way her grandmother used to when she was praying over one of her many hurts.

"But you were in your element with that audience. They loved you."

"They loved the surprise because they were the first to know. That's what they were attracted to."

"So their response had nothing to do with you."

"Sure, I was the catalyst, but I could have been anybody. If a famous man who'd been missing for two years suddenly walked out of the desert, wouldn't he cause a big splash?"

"Don't think you're worth turning a few heads?"

"Yes." Her lips were full and thick and made for smiling. While she worked, she licked them and took her time answering him. "Beauty fades over time. That audience didn't care about my accomplishments outside modeling, my social beliefs or my political views. They simply wanted the show."

"I'm still confused as to how you can see their reaction to you and not want to respond. I'm confused about how you can touch me, and make me scared as hell to touch you."

"I don't mean to be confusing. After all you did for me today, I *do* feel differently. But I'm a realist," she said, meeting his gaze solidly. Ebony lashes fluttered against her cheeks and she shouldered her hair out of the way. "My change of heart can only be in terms of how we act toward one another professionally. You didn't deserve my hostility."

She wiped her hands on the towel on the floor and rubbed her palm against his thigh. Suddenly she stopped.

"Rob, two years, five months ago, my mother died, and with her, so did my passion." Loren sat on the divan, Rob's left leg on the floor, his right leg resting on the pads on the sofa.

"I didn't want to leave the house. I didn't want to model, I didn't want to eat. I didn't want to make love. I just wanted to sleep."

"You were depressed. Did you see a doctor?"

"No. I had shows in Milan and New York and there was no time. He—" she jerked her head toward the TV and Rob knew she was talking about Odesi "—wanted me to snap out of it. He kept saying 'It's the cycle of life.' I knew that. But she was everything to me. We were closer than mother and daughter. We were like sisters."

"Were you with her?"

Loren shook her head. "I was in Monaco and she was here decorating my brand-new apartment. She'd gone shopping at the mall and fell down an escalator off a curb and hit her head. It's the stupidest way to die. She was so young." Loren tried to staunch the flow of tears, but they spilled over and she held the towel to her eyes for a few seconds. "I miss her," she signed.

A big breath later she put the towel down and saw his hands. She looked at him and shook her head. Rob thought of withdrawing them when Loren moved the divan closer.

He kept his hands out, but she was scared. Overcoming her fear, she put her hands in his and looked him in the eye.

"I'd already confronted Odesi about the pictures of the women he'd taken advantage of, and he still felt I should make love to him. I wanted to leave. To be alone in my grief for my mother, but he wouldn't have it. He stabbed me six times because I wouldn't give in to him. He thought it was about him and it wasn't. He wouldn't believe me when I said I couldn't."

"That's insane. Did you have surgery? Are you better?"

She shook her head. "They did their best. The scars are on my abdomen. I know there's a surgery that can remove all the old scars and scar tissue, but it's expensive."

"That's why you need the money."

Loren nodded. "I have money, but I'm afraid to touch it

because I'd planned the surgery once before and he found out and was there in the parking lot when I arrived. I was so afraid I went into hiding. Not even Zoe knew where I was. You're right about the fire forcing me out of hiding, but I'm not dead."

"If what you say is on that flash drive, then he's as good as gotten. It's just a matter of time. Is that why you keep a bag packed? You're always ready to run."

"Yes. Yes." The tears poured out of her then. "I'm scared. That's why I stay inside. I'm scared he'll get me."

"He won't because I'm going to get him."

The tears spilled over and he wiped them with the towel. Rob rubbed her hand again.

"Your first night here you walked in with a bag. You had credit cards, and you have car keys in the waist of your pants at all times. Most people that escape fires only get out with the clothes on their backs."

"Rob, he's hurt women from around the world, and he's never been caught. I believe he wants me gone so he can continue to be free, that's why I'm so afraid to be in public. Besides his father, I knew everything about him, and I could ruin his career and his life. He just doesn't realize that if he leaves me alone, I won't bother him."

"You can't live your life like that."

"I keep thinking he's going to come back, so I have to be ready to get away."

"He's not coming here, Loren."

The tears were gone and he still had her hands. "You don't know him. He can do anything he wants. Diplomatic immunity is like a platinum card."

"Odesi's a diplomat, too?"

"No, only his father. He's the ambassador to Lagos."

"And the immunity extends to his son?"

Loren nodded. "Yes, because he's taking over his father's position in a few months. He's untouchable."

"Not to Hoods. You can trust me."

"Rob," she said with a sigh, "men have promised to help me—investigators, cops, government officials. Some have disappeared. Others just stopped taking my calls." She gave a thoughtful pause. "But I have to give you credit. No one has done more for me than you and your family."

"I can promise to help you get your life back, Lakota. I can be honest and tell you I want to know more about you than sitting here in this house."

Loren drew back, his words seeming to surprise her. "He will go to any length to get to me, including killing you. His freedom means that much to him. No, Rob. Not for Zoe or Ben's sake. Not for me. This is my life and my fight, and I choose to give up. Now, please help me get it back on track, but don't go after him. If you do, I'll disappear and you'll never see me again."

Chapter 12

The words rushed out of her and he still held her hands, because he seemed to know if he let go she'd fly away like one of the hummingbirds that frequented Zoe's yard. Still, he wasn't afraid. Not of her fear and not of Odesi. She'd never met a man like Rob before. He wasn't overconfident, bolstered by drugs or fame. She was sitting with a regular man who was growing by extraordinary leaps in her eyes.

"Loren, I've caught more bad men in my lifetime than I care to admit. Any man who hits a woman is a coward, and I'm not scared of that type of man. I need to tell you something, and I want you to get angry and then it's over."

She tensed despite his words. "What did you do?"

"I bought you some baking supplies. You can repay me if you want or I'll take them home when I go. I know you have to cook for the restaurant and I wanted you to have what you needed."

He'd planned and executed the ultimate "welcome back from the dead" event for her, had respected all her rules, and everything had gone off without a hitch, and here she sat, laying all his troubles at his feet. Now he'd tied the ultimate knot on the package so why *was* she angry? No one told him to go ahead and buy her things.

She looked everywhere but at him. Anger heated the bottom of her feet, moved through her body to her palms and ended in her eyes. She could feel them narrow. Odesi used to clear the room when she was furious at him. Rob went on as though her burning holes in him with her eyes meant nothing.

"I also called the bank. We'll need to go over there tomorrow, but they're going to have to issue you new cards just as a precaution."

"I didn't ask you to do that."

"Yes, you did. You said 'I need your help. They cut off my credit cards,' and I assumed you meant help with everything."

His hands held hers tighter, and the anger seemed to drop off her in chunks. "No, no. You're right." She saw the birch trees being rustled by the wind and wished she was out there. "You *have* helped me. Your whole family. I've never seen anything like that before, except when I lived with Mother in South Dakota."

She was not engulfed by fury anymore, but helplessness and longing. "When will the supplies be here?" she asked.

"In about an hour."

"How much was everything, Rob?"

"Nine hundred dollars."

Their gazes locked, held. "What did you buy?" she exploded. "Emeril's cookware?"

He nodded.

She leaned her elbows on her knees and looked off to the side and shook her hands. He still wouldn't let go. "I don't know what to say. I should be doing something else for you. Thank you. I'll write you a check."

"You're welcome. And no, you don't have to."

"I don't know why you're…"

"Yes, you do, Lakota. Don't go backward. I think we need each other equally."

"I need to be alone."

"No, you don't. You want to go outside and I need to."

"Stop reading my thoughts. Stop telling me what I'm feeling

before I can fix it in my mind. Stop helping me before I know I need help," she said impatiently. "Stop being so nice to me."

He caressed the back of her hand. "You're making it so easy, darlin'. I would like to ask a favor."

How could she deny him? Loren sighed, unable to be angry with him. "What is it?"

"My birthday is in two days. Will you have dinner with me?"

"Don't you want to spend the day with your family?"

He shook his head. "Since DeLinda died, things like this turn real solemn and my family doesn't know how to handle it. They try really hard to be upbeat, but it's forced, so I don't do anything. This year I decided I would break that pattern."

She felt steadier now that she could help him. "I'll cook for you. What would you like?"

"Anything you fix will be fine with me. A cupcake, too. Any flavor, but I'm partial to chocolate."

She smiled. "Just one?"

"I don't want to look at a cake the next day." He was sure of what he wanted, and a calm assurance surrounded them. She felt as if she understood him. Loren found herself liking Rob more than she'd ever thought possible.

"One cupcake it is. How's your leg?"

"It's okay. Better, I think."

"Since you ordered supplies, I want to bake. The kitchen is off-limits to you."

"I have to eat, woman. I've been working hard all day and all you've brought me is this dirt and water."

She paused and tried not to laugh. "Your colon will be clean if you drink your tea."

He handed it to her. "My colon is just fine, thank you. My leg feels good, too, thanks."

"You're welcome. Stay off of it."

Rob looked at her as he rested his head on the back of the sofa. "I guess I should call my sisters over here to cook for me."

The smile slipped away and she looked into her bowl of massage oil. "I'll feed you or you can try a better bribe tomorrow, you sorry bum."

Rob burst out laughing. "What am I supposed to do? Ask you to cook for me today and for my birthday?" He paused. "You scare me, Lakota Sky."

"I could say the same for you."

"I've never scared a woman. Not even my wife."

Their gazes locked. "You miss her."

He nodded.

"I know about that."

"I know you do," he said.

"What most?" Loren put the bowls on the counter and returned to the den. She had to know. Rob intrigued her as much as he scared her. There was something about him that made her feel very much alive, and like a woman.

He had such a respect for his deceased wife, a gentle esteem that Loren found endearing and honorable. While he'd been holding her hands, he'd been caressing them, his fingers linking with hers. The reassurance she'd felt was comforting and she'd missed that feeling of wholeness. At one point, she'd wanted to join him on the sofa and sit right beside him, and she hadn't ever entertained that thought. Rob Hood was different from any man she'd known and that made her want to know him more. She wanted to know about his life and his past in his own words. He was right here and willing to talk.

"I hope I'm not prying too much. Perhaps I am. I'm sorry."

"I'm glad you asked. Everyone assumes when a spouse dies you love them forever, and can't open your heart to love again, and that's not true. I miss the loving aspects of the relationship, of course. The companionship. Talking every day. Television shows we had in common. Family get-togethers and outings."

Despite herself, Loren blushed. She didn't quite meet his gaze and gathered the towel and pad. "What are you hungry for?" she said quietly.

"Would a better answer have been I miss talking about balancing the checkbook?"

A quick smile claimed her before she could stop it. "No, of course not." She shrugged and looked away.

"Why are you embarrassed? Your face is so red." He thumbed her cheek.

"You miss the showers, right?"

He nodded and started laughing. "We never showered together. I've always wanted to do that."

"You never showered together?" Loren couldn't imagine. Even her mother and father had done that. "Italians love that. In Italy, my boyfriend and I used to walk in the rain."

His brows furrowed. "You were ten!"

Loren smacked his hand. "You nut. I didn't have sex at ten. I've been back to Italy since then." She paused. "I see what you're doing. You're not funny."

"You're laughing," he said, and pushed her knees as he chuckled. "So you like walking in the rain."

"Well, not in Georgia. You'll get struck by lightning. But yes, in Italy, I could see doing that with my spouse. What else? Music?"

"Music is universal," he said. "You like jazz. I like jazz, hip-hop, R & B, rap. It's all good. I *miss* being with a woman."

He looked at her and she could feel her face turn red again. Loren touched her cheeks.

"In modeling, men were crass. Sex talk was harsh and vulgar for the most part. You said 'I miss being with a woman' like, 'Can I have hummus on my sandwich?'"

This time he really laughed, and she couldn't help but smile and knock his good knee. "What's so funny, Rob?"

"I didn't mean it that way. I just meant I miss the physical pleasure of making love. Any healthy adult loves making love, and for the record, I never want hummus on my sandwich."

"You miss it just with her?"

"No." His gaze penetrated deep into her, farther than anything she'd ever known. Her insides shook and she felt her heart beat stronger. She allowed him access to a point, then she willed his hold to be broken. "The love I had for her remains with her because I know she'll never return."

"That's beautiful, Rob."

He nodded.

"And you're ready to move on?"

"I've been ready for a long time."

"With me?" she whispered.

He moved the pad and towel. "I'd like that."

"I wouldn't be some rebound woman."

He shook his head. "Never. I have dated since I've been single."

"How many?" she asked softly.

"Two," he smiled. "And you?"

She shook her head. "None. Well, I babysat for my neighbors on New Year's Eve while I was in Italy. Their son is fifteen and their daughter is ten." She shrugged. "Hanging out with kids counts as none, I suppose."

Rob grinned. "I'll give you half a date for the daughter and half a date for the son."

She swept her hair behind her ear and dragged her fingers slowly through to the ends. "Thanks. My grand total is one."

"We can start over together."

She thought about it for a moment and then tried to get up. "I think you're hungry."

"I am, Lakota. For you. Not just sexually. To be your friend."

All the air in the room seemed to gather in her lungs. She shook her head. "Just so you can have sex with me?"

He frowned so distastefully, she wished she'd kept her mouth shut. "If I ever have children, they will never model. That demented business has warped your mind. I want to know you. Your mind and your heart. What you like and don't like. What makes you laugh. What your goals are. I want to know how to love you."

Skepticism and curiosity could not occupy the same space. She knew both played out in equal measure across her face because Rob caressed her hair and caught the ends between his fingers. They both stared at the strands that had been sheared in an even line not more than a week ago in her bathroom.

"Never heard that before?" His thumb played her hair like an accordion.

"No. I don't know how I feel about it, either." She blinked, watching his thumb, breathing his air, wondering what to do next.

"You want me to know about you."

"Why are you so sure about that?" she asked, flicking her hair from between his fingers.

"Because," he said, bringing her close. "It's about living in the moment."

"What are you going to do?" she asked.

"Nothing. What are you going to do, Loren?"

Loren gathered her strength and wanted to push away, but couldn't. She felt as if the wind from outside was guiding her closer to him, and in a second their lips touched. The simple pleasure was so tender, she groaned and leaned into Rob, her hand on the back of his neck.

His mouth was welcome and warm from the tea, and she liked

the feel of what she'd been missing so long. More than anything, she wanted to be in his arms, and he seemed to sense that. He held her until she remembered she was supposed to be keeping her distance. She stepped back and looked at her shoes.

"You're hungry. I'll get you something right away." Loren walked into the kitchen, leaving him in the den. Standing in the pantry, she covered her chest with her arms and tried to still the desire to be with him. Rob was making a good case to make love without even asking.

Using his crutches, he came into the kitchen behind her. "Canned soup is fine with me."

She regarded him from the pantry. "Rob, you're speaking to a chef, who claims American, Indian and Italian as her strongest culinary influences. Nothing I cook comes from a can. Why don't you sit down? I can fix you something to eat and bring it to you."

"If you're cooking, I'm watching. I've got nothing better to do."

"Watch TV."

An embarrassed expression crossed his forehead and settled on his cheeks. "I never figured out how to get the TV working, just the radio. That's part of the reason I ended up in the upstairs bedroom. The TV in the bedroom down here is just like this one."

She scoffed. "Your man card is in jeopardy."

"No, it's not, baby."

Her body responded and she turned toward him. Her breasts pushed against her top and she had to resist doing anything suggestive. She was terribly attracted to Rob. Though she'd sworn off men, her body wasn't being so cooperative. In the past twenty-four hours, she'd been craving intimacy and not with just anyone. Just Rob.

Initially he had the opposite effect on her, but at the studio today, as she'd mingled with the guests after the show, she found herself constantly looking for him. A couple of times she'd laughed and she'd seen him watching her. He'd always smiled, his eyebrow oddly arched, his body attuned to hers. Just knowing that he'd sparked her interest scared her to death. Discovering now that he wanted to know all about her made her want to tell him.

She wanted to tell him about learning the language of the Lakota, growing up multiracial, loving her parents and missing them so. She wanted to *talk* to him. But he had all the power in the world to hurt her and she couldn't let that happen. "I'm not your baby."

"Is there something wrong with me being affectionate with you?" he asked.

"I don't like the false implication of intimacy."

She said it to deflect him, but he didn't move, as if her words didn't have any effect on him at all.

"What we just shared wasn't false, and you know it. Let your guard down just a little. I promise not to hurt you, but you have to want to know me, too, and I think you do."

She opened the refrigerator and put meat on the table, along with potatoes, when Rob's cell phone rang, ending any further response.

"Rob Hood."

The doorbell rang and Loren took the opportunity to escape. Grabbing her defense spray, she walked past Rob and, though cautious, took delivery of the packages.

The bright morning had birthed a lovely summer day, with children playing in the street, and fathers talking to the others near their cars at the end of the driveway. She missed her dad as much as she missed her mom, and she stood outside long enough to fill her lungs full of the sun before the brown truck pulled away.

That's when she noticed the out-of-place black town car six cars down. What place did it have between a Range Rover and a purple minivan, a foot from the curb? Several fathers with their toddlers in the neighborhood noticed it, too.

Loren dragged a box inside, leaving the others at the door. Rob was standing there with his shorts on, unaware of the distraction he presented.

"Rob, the pots are here. And there's a town car outside that wasn't there before—"

Loren put the box down to look at the paper he was rustling.

"They've got a new suspect in my wife's murder," he said in a hushed tone, still listening to the caller. "Five murders of Indian women in the area when DeLinda died."

He grabbed the back of her hand and kissed it, then caught her in a big hug that was so spontaneous and warm Loren allowed it. "Thank you, Lakota. Thank you."

Chapter 13

"Guys, I'll call you back." Rob hung up, dropping his phone on the sofa in a gentle movement, his gaze never leaving hers.

"You were just talking about her. How can you hold me this way?"

He could feel her insecurity, but he also saw the desire in her eyes to be held. Loren never pulled away. When he called her Lakota, she turned into him. She needed affection and he wanted to give it to her. Her help led them to this development and his heart was full for her.

"I'm finishing what I started." Rob held Loren against him, his strong arms bringing her body firmly against his. "Thank you for your help. They've got someone, and the detectives are close to a confession. This case will be closed because of your help, Lakota."

"Oh, Rob." When she hugged him, he could tell she meant it. "I'm so glad for you. So it's over."

All of Rob's attention was focused on the woman in his arms. He felt free for the first time in years. "Yes, it's over."

She moved to step back, but he didn't quite let her go. "And you're free to—"

"I'm free to do whatever I want. I've been free for a long time, Lakota. I want you to know that. That other chapter of my life is now closed. I'm very attracted to you, Lakota Sky Thunderhawk. I can't go backward. My heart is open to you. If you let me, I'd kiss you right now."

Rob drank in the sight of her, thankful for the strides they'd made in the weeks they'd been together. She was ready to come out of her cocoon and he wanted her to want him.

"I'm, uh…flattered." She didn't quite smile, but she licked her lips, catching her bottom lip between her teeth and then letting it go. "You make me nervous."

"Why?"

"Because you stand so close to me." She spoke softly as her lashes fluttered against her cheeks.

Rob nodded. "When a person is nervous, they shift their feet and their heart races. They shake and stutter. They're even breathless. You're none of those things. Are you?"

She wouldn't look him in the eye, but kept her gaze on his lips as she shook her head. "No."

"Because?"

She blinked quickly. "I don't know." She pushed back, looking as if she was getting ready to run. "Because I have to face the truth."

Her words shocked him. "What is your truth? What do you want?"

She didn't look away and she didn't move. "To know what it's like to be wanted."

His heart leaped and he nearly swept her off her feet, but he maintained strict control of himself. "Kiss me, Lakota. Not like before. Like you really mean it."

Her exhalation brushed his lips and she shook her head again. "I can't."

"Why?" he asked, lacing his fingers with hers, bringing her closer.

"Because you want to kiss me."

A full smile bloomed. Holding her, he guided her head to his chest and kissed her cheek.

Her eyes sprang open and she blinked several times.

Rob wasn't sure what she was going to say or do, but he didn't move and neither did she. She was in need of care, in need of love, and he had so much to give. He knew she did, too. He just felt it. Nestling her in his arms, he softly bathed her cheek in kisses. Rob knew he couldn't dance, but he did his best one-legged sway as he caressed her back and kissed her cheek.

A fraction at a time, she moved and he finally kissed her nose. She shook a little, as if a slice of thunder rippled through her body, but she didn't back away. She pressed her shoulders a little closer into him, her face angling up just a little more, her eyes open, looking at him.

Her eyelashes were coal-dark, gleaming with just a hint of moisture. He touched his lips to hers. Then looked at her again. Her tongue snaked out and glided across her lips, and Rob felt himself falling in love with her. Their lips touched again and their souls finally said hello. His hand got lost in her hair and their mouths met again. He couldn't help closing his eyes. He felt his romantic heart sinking into the kiss as his mouth moved gently over hers. Nothing else mattered, not her former super-model status, not her sex appeal, just the fact that he was so close to Lakota and was breathing her air.

Her hands were on his arms and he felt her fingers graze his cheek. It was too soon to take her to bed, but he wanted to show her how a real man loved a real woman. Her lips parted and their tongues met.

Rob could feel the groan deep in his body as it woke up and rumbled out of him. She caught it in her mouth, letting it curl around her tongue, her eyes half closed. Rob watched this natural beauty, and sank his mouth onto hers again, his tongue stroking the top of her mouth, catching her moan in his body. He couldn't believe he'd ever spent a moment not knowing this kiss or those lips. A blaring horn broke the spell that bound them.

Furious yells caught their attention and they both hurried to the sunroom. "The men on the street are angry," Loren said.

Rob hurried to his computer in time to see a town car roll past the house.

"How'd you get that on your computer?"

"My cousin Hugh was a very busy man while we were gone. He installed cameras outside to make sure we know what's going on and are never taken by surprise."

Loren was looking at the neighbors. Some of the men were writing down the license plate of the fleeing car. They took Neighborhood Watch seriously around here. "This is so high-tech," she said.

Rob was glad to finally impress her. "It is. I'll get the license number when they call it in to the police. I can't go out there and ask them for it because they don't know me."

"I met the gentlemen when Zoe moved in. I can ask them," she offered.

Rob shook his head. "No. That can lead to someone getting hurt. The fewer people who know your schedule or that you're definitely here, the better."

"Do you think that was Odesi?" Loren picked up another box from the door.

"No. You just did the interview. I don't want you to start worrying. I'm positive that no one knows for sure that you're in here. No one can hear inside this house. Hugh took care of that while he was here."

Loren stopped. "Who are you people? You appear out of thin air and then you disappear. There's a lot of you. Did your family procreate like normal or are you robots?"

"If I told you, I'd have to—"

"Kill me. That's such a ridiculous statement."

"Who's trying to ruin my fun? I want to kiss you. All night long."

She regarded him and walked a wider path back to the front door. "Stay where you are or I'll take that knee out," she said, and brought back another box. "I think we've done enough kissing for one day."

"You don't think that." He went back to the couch and sat down.

"How do you know what I'm thinking?"

"Your body says differently."

"You don't know my body." Her glance was hesitant, her words not quite defensive, but Rob decided to let things go before she completely shut him out.

Loren sat across the room and started to open the boxes. He'd forgotten how much he missed the joy of watching a woman. She assessed everything with her eyes, and her mouth was her most expressive feature. She puckered her lips.

"These are beautiful. I've always wanted this." She admired the pans, caressing the finish.

"If you don't mind my saying so, you have money. Why didn't you just buy them?"

"You can't have everything in life, Rob. There are things I want more, like privacy."

"What do you do with all that private time? Walk around your house naked?"

A burst of laughter shot out of her and she blushed. "None of your business."

Rob watched as she adjusted her T-shirt to make sure she wasn't showing any skin. *So she didn't walk around naked.* She didn't push her hair behind her ear, letting it shield her face from him. Well, that was going to change if she was going to be in his life. His family knew to call before they visited because he believed in being undressed as often as possible.

Loren's cell phone rang. "Maybe that's the bank. Hello?"

Rob went to the window and studied where the town car had

been parked on the street. He had no doubt in his mind it had been her ex's or his father's. Someone had been looking for Loren and had found her. Not only was his job to keep her safe, but he would catch the person and make them sorry they'd gone to the trouble of disturbing her peace.

Dialing his phone, he called Hugh with the update and gave an assessment also. When he hung up, Rob put some weight on his knee and felt the tenderness. He was supposed to have more strength by now. He needed to see the doctor about his leg.

"No, Dionne," he heard Loren say. "I don't want to model again. I just feel that time in my life is over. What designers have called you?"

Loren's laugh ran up and down his skin like a warm breeze. He loved hearing it. She'd gone into the dining room and was standing in the mirror, looking critically at strands of her hair.

Rob unpacked pots and put them onto the table. What woman wouldn't be flattered that designers were calling for her to model for them? Loren said she wasn't. She *was* unusual.

"Vera?" she sounded surprised. "She never wanted me before. Sure, I'm flattered," she said with that exotic accent he was sure she'd taken some ribbing over as a child. "I just don't want that life, Dionne. What walk? Oh, I made that up right then. I've gained a little weight, so gliding was better for my body type. A TV show? Sure, I'll think about it. No magazine layouts," Loren said firmly. "I will *not* show the scars to anyone. Look, I've got to go. Let me call you next week. A friend is recuperating and I'm helping him, so I can't be disturbed. I've got money, thank you, darling." Her voice softened. "Really, you're very kind to offer. Love to you, Dionne."

Rob pulled the third box onto the table and opened it, expecting Loren to come into the kitchen. He tested his knee and sucked wind through his teeth at the pain.

After it passed, he called the doctor's office. "It's Rob Hood.

I had knee-replacement surgery and something snapped about an hour ago." He made an appointment for later that afternoon.

"I'll take it, thanks." He went to the door of the dining room and stuck his head in.

"Hi." Loren leaned over the phone book as she dialed, then against the wall, bringing her cell phone to her ear. "This is Loren Smith. I'd like to speak to Lieutenant Heath, please."

She waved Rob in, but he shook his head, signing that he needed a ride to the doctor.

She nodded, her eyes bright. "Lieutenant? It's Loren Smith. You saved me from my apartment fire. Yes, it's me. I didn't make you famous. You're a real hero."

Rob could hear her laughing as he pulled the pans from the boxes and put them on the table. "Please don't apologize about the misunderstanding about me being dead. It's not your fault. I'm getting that straightened out. Sure I'll hold." Loren hummed, then cleared her throat. "Yes, I'm here," she said. "The fire marshal gave his approval? That's wonderful. I was starting to get worried because it's been two weeks. Sure, I'll stop by the station and give autographs." She paused. "That much was salvageable? I'll make arrangements for a moving truck. Thank you, Lieutenant. What's your company number? Six. Sure, I'd be glad to. Yes, I'll hold. Rob?" she called.

He entered the doorway, and Loren was sitting with her foot on the chair, holding the phone, her elbows on the table.

"Yes?"

"Come here. You've got to hear this. I promised to thank the firefighters. I'll put the phone on speaker. Lieutenant Heath will be back in a second."

Rob maneuvered the chair and sat beside her. He didn't think she realized she'd taken his hand, but she had. Her palm was smooth and capable as she pressed hers into his.

"Loren," the lieutenant said. "We're all assembled."

"Company Six, thank you for saving my life."

"Ma'am, yes, ma'am!"

She and Rob burst out laughing at their cheers.

"Lieutenant, and Company Six, I'll come by tomorrow and bring you all something special."

Another cheer filled the dining room, making them smile.

"Thanks, and, Loren, we're buddies now. Call me Tim."

"Thanks, Tim. Goodbye."

She disconnected the call and saw that her hand was intertwined with Rob's. "Hey, you reached for me," he told her, defending himself before she beat him up.

"Well, don't get crazy—"

He stopped her midsentence. "You know I had a hard lesson to learn after DeLinda died."

Loren gazed at their fingers. "What was it?"

"Not to be destructive to the people around me. You can like holding my hand."

"I don't want you to think it means anything."

"Because meaning something would be wrong, right? When you don't think, you're so much better at being nice." Rob winced at his own words. "I can call Hugh to take me to the doctor."

"I said I'd take you."

"That was before you caught yourself holding my hand."

She got up and walked a couple of feet away. "Trust is a long road, Rob. I don't mean to take you through all the bumpy parts with me."

There were rent-a-car businesses on every corner near the airport. He wondered if there were rent-a-psychologist offices nearby. He'd known Loren for just a few days and sometimes he wanted to shake her, other times he wanted to make love to her, but he found himself wanting to love her. Still, he wasn't sure what would fix her.

"Woman, you confuse the hell out of me."

To earn a Lakota Sky smile was like finding a penny worth a hundred dollars. And he got one. A beautiful smile that rivaled any other.

"I'm sorry. Okay, a kiss on your birthday."

"You're kidding." He clutched his chest.

Loren blushed. "I don't kid about such things. I need to go to the store and get cooking supplies. If we take your chair, will you go with me?"

"I hate that chair."

"If we get one of those motor chairs in the store, will you please go with me?"

Her eyes pleaded. Her shoulders were up and she was braced for him to say no. The fact that she knew she had to go out and was willing to go was a big step in the right direction as far as he was concerned. "I'll go with you. For a handshake."

"That will seal our agreement? A handshake. I thought…"

"You thought what?"

"Nothing." She extended her hand.

Rob took her hand and, in very slow motion, gave her the soul brother handshake. She began to smile as she watched his fingers curl with hers at the end. Then his fingers tiptoed toward her elbow. "What do you want right now, Loren?"

She watched his fingers on her arm. "Another hug. Just like before."

Rob leaned against the table and slowly brought her to him. His arms circled her waist and he held her not too closely, but close enough so that he felt her against him. He closed his eyes and reveled in the feel of her.

"A little tighter, please," she said.

He was practicing so much restraint that he was glad to relax and hold her the ways she wanted him to.

Her hair felt like silk against his chin, and she unconsciously scratched his back in a way that aroused him. "Are you good?" he asked.

"One more minute."

She was like a baby. A contented six-foot baby that was finally soothed.

But she was a woman, and there was so much more that he wanted from her. A minute passed and then two. "We can pick this up later," he said, trying to leave the erotic expectation out of his voice.

"Okay."

Shock prickled him. He waited for the other shoe to drop.

"But this doesn't mean I—"

"You like me." Rob finished the sentence, making her laugh. "One day your broken record isn't going to play. I'm glad liking me isn't a prerequisite to hugging me."

She bit her lip and started for the kitchen.

"Are we still on for breakfast, because I'm starving."

"Yes, I'm hungry, too." Loren's calmness gave him hope. "Then let's go before we get into trouble."

Chapter 14

At the grocery store, Loren was recognized. What should have taken forty-five minutes took two hours. She signed autographs and posed for cell-phone pictures. At times it was an effort, but she was patient and always kind.

By the time they got to the doctor's office, Rob thought they would reschedule him.

But the second they saw Loren, Rob was an afterthought. Even his friend Dr. Leonard Dillard was enthralled. "Rob, are you seeing her?"

"Living with. We're housemates."

Len's black-framed glasses slid down his nose, exposing wide dark eyes and bushy eyebrows. "How'd you get so lucky?"

"Family," he told the doc. "What happened to my knee?"

"Nothing. You're fine."

"Doc, it hurts."

"I told you to stay off the stairs. But you're not, are you?"

"No."

"There you go. You're overusing the joint. It popped realigning itself. Let it heal and you'll have this knee for another sixty years."

"You said seventy after the surgery."

The doctor was still looking at Loren, who was charming other patients across the gym. Since their exam was complete, he'd moved Rob to the gym with the other patients and was using heat and ice therapy.

"I did say seventy, but you wore off ten taking the stairs before you were supposed to. You won't live another seventy years, anyway." He patted Rob's back and crossed his arms, staring at Loren. "She's gorgeous."

Rob elbowed him. "You're lucky I know what a clown you are."

Doc Dillard turned to Rob. "You've got the best replacement knee possible. But you have to respect it. Incidental stair usage for the next week. Not up and down every ten minutes. Get out and walk on level ground and do your exercises. I'll release you in three weeks if you don't have any further setbacks."

"You said two last week."

"That was before the big pop. But if nothing else happens, I'll surprise you."

"Someone is being hardheaded, I see," Loren said. "May I?"

Rob patted the space on the workout table next to him and Loren eased up, leaving a little space between them.

The doctor spun around, his hand out. "Leonard Dillard. I'm your biggest fan."

Loren glanced at Rob as if to say 'Is he for real'?

"Doc, she doesn't like to touch people."

"Me, neither." The doc folded his hands and then shoved them in his doctor's coat.

She extended her hand and he shook it effusively. "I'm okay," she told Rob.

"I was trying to save you," Rob warned Loren. "How can you say you don't like touching people, Len? You performed my surgery."

"Oh, that. Well, that's for the beach house Sandy wants. But if Loren agrees to marry me, I'll leave Sandy."

Rob and Loren laughed at Leonard's nerdish demeanor. He strolled in front of them, his lips moving as he did math computations in the air with his finger. Thinking seemed to have burned a railroad track down the center of his head, but Len didn't care. He wore the rest of the curly mane about four inches high and won his patients over with his self-deprecating humor and his obvious brilliance.

"Len, what about my godchildren?" Rob only added fuel to the fire.

"Oh, them. She can have them. They're not mine, anyway."

"Kiley looks just like you." Rob playfully elbowed Loren.

Len shook his head. "Sweet kid, but no she doesn't."

Loren's smile was beautiful. She had caught on that they were good friends. "Leonard, I was there for both baby showers," Rob reminded him. "They're your kids, too."

"Sandy throws it in my face that they're blond like her." The doc shook his head. "Loren, I'm dark-haired, you're dark-haired. You're not really a blonde, are you?"

"No." She smiled, moving closer to Rob when Len tried to see her roots. "Natural brunette."

"Good. Wanna marry me? I overcharge people like Rob here," he half whispered as if Rob couldn't hear. "So when a fox like you shows up, I can get my stash of fifty-five hundred dollars and we can take off. It's not a lot, but I've got a car, and a ten-speed bike from the early seventies, and lunch the kids packed for me. We could be happy if we camped out a lot."

"Dr. Dillard, Sandy and the kids on line two," the receptionist said over the intercom.

"Damn her. I can't have any fun."

"I simply cannot break up your happy home, but thank you." Loren pretended to look sad for Len's benefit.

He stomped. "I get that all the time. I'll be back."

They watched him go. Loren had wrapped her hand around Rob's arm. He knew it was costing her to be in public, but he was grateful for her bravery. He didn't mind that she was using him for support. Len was actually helping her become acclimated to being in public again with his zany sense of humor.

"He's hilarious," Loren said. "Where'd you find him?"

"Eighth grade."

"You're kidding."

"No. He was the smartest kid in my chemistry class. We went to high school together and have stayed in touch. He's always been funny. Where are your high school friends?"

"I don't know. Zoe is my only friend and she's from my college days. That's it."

"Why not anyone else?"

"When you do what I've done, people get jealous and fall away. Or they get tired of you not being able to participate in the important events in their lives. It's actually quite understandable. You make friends in the business you're in, and the others either understand and wait, or they leave you alone and sell your story for a few dollars later."

"That's awful. I'd beat someone's—"

"Watch that mouth," she warned.

"I'm watching it, baby."

The doctor returned to the gym with an aide, who fitted Rob with a less-cumbersome knee brace and a cane, and he hobbled to the room and changed from gym shorts to jeans. Returning, he accepted prescriptions and a sample of cream for his knee.

"How many pain pills do you have left?" Doc Dillard asked.

Rob handed him the bottle. "I think twelve."

"You were supposed to be taking one per day."

"As needed," Rob emphasized. "I didn't need them every day."

"Your muscles are healing. Your brain might not think it needs them, but your muscles do."

"I get too sleepy when I take them, Len. I can't think straight."

Dr. Dillard regarded him. "Rob, I'm going to suggest you take the over-the-counter pain reliever every four hours for three days. You're healing nicely, but I want the muscles to relax at night when you're sleeping. That's when most of the healing takes place. Also, this brace is lighter and you'll have more mobility."

"When can I get off these crutches?"

"A week. Walk every day. Outside," Len emphasized. "Now, in a week, you use the cane. Seven days, Loren, do you hear me? Not six, but seven days. Rob, you must walk every day. Do the exercises I sent home with you."

"Don't say things like that in front of her," Rob told him. "She gets bossy."

Leonard patted his shoulder, then hugged him. "Come here, you big bear. I'm so glad you have a girlfriend."

"Len, get off me before you start crying, and she's not my girlfriend."

"You always were a little dumb, but I still love you, man. She's your girlfriend if you smarten up."

Loren watched them as if she were studying specimens. Except she never stopped smiling.

Rob regarded him. "Len, are you blubbering on my shirt?"

Len was still hugging him. "There's nothing wrong with a man having a tender heart. That's why Sandy loves me. Loren, do you know the fairy tale of Robin Hood?"

"No. Lakota Indians don't really have much interest in English tales."

"I can see where that might not be of much significance to your people. Well, you should get Rob to tell you how he tore up this knee. He was doing something truly good."

"Doc—" Rob's tone held a warning. Loren was practically

under his thigh and Len was blowing his nose. Rob just wanted to get out of there.

"I'm here because my body is getting old. Now, if you know the intersection of the fountain of youth and wealth, tell me. I'll stop by there first. Otherwise we've got to go. Loren and I have plans."

"If I knew that intersection I'd be selling tickets instead of doing this dead-end job." He sighed heavily, and Loren's chest shook in laughter against his arm. Rob's thoughts could hardly stay focused.

The doc returned from Never Land. "Rob, use the knee, but no running, no catching bad guys. Oh, and Sandy sends her love, by the way. Oh, and she said to tell you she's knocked up again by the mailman."

This time Loren's breast brushed his arm when she laughed, and Rob pulled his lips into his mouth, glad Loren was beside him.

"Come back in three weeks," the doc told Rob.

Rob headed for the door and Loren walked with the paperwork and cane, waving goodbye to everyone. "Your friend is a funny man. He should do stand-up comedy."

"He was charming because of you."

Loren shook her head. "I watched him study your X-rays and look at measurements to make sure your knee is healing properly."

"He's the best in his field." Loren had adjusted her stride to match his step and soon they were at the car. He sank into her station wagon and shoved his crutches in the back. He was glad his knee was healing, but unhappy that he'd suffered a setback. "I don't want to go home."

The new brace did feel better and gave him more mobility, but he could feel his mood sinking. *A week longer because he hadn't done as he'd been told. Stay off the stairs.*

They left DeKalb Orthopedic Rehab Center and headed toward Stone Mountain. Loren made a right onto Ponce de Leon. "Where are we going? Do you want to go home? I have all this food. What do you want to do?"

"Just drive for a little while."

"Some of it needs to be refrigerated."

"Take this street and make a right. We'll go another two miles and hit a service station. I'll get a cooler and some ice." Down the road, Rob thought to lower the window. "Do you mind?" he asked.

She glanced at him. "No."

The summer heat had broken its hold on the September day and yielded to a fall breeze that was spectacular. Rob closed his eyes for a few minutes and tried to do some of that creative visualization Xan was often trying to get him to buy into, but he couldn't shake the overriding feeling of being less than the best. He rubbed his knee. There was titanium in his leg. He was never going to be the same, but he knew he had to get past it.

Loren pulled into the service station, put on sunglasses and a baseball cap.

"I'll get the cooler." Rob reached into the backseat for his crutches. He was at least good for something.

"You heard the doctor. You watch for criminals so they don't steal Betsy," she said, referring to the car. "I'll be right back."

"Yeah, okay." An unexpected laugh trickled out. He was a good lookout man. "I don't know what the demand is for Betsy."

"What? This station wagon is vintage, I'll have you know."

"It's a classic," he corrected.

"That's right, and you've been riding in style all day, so don't hate on my baby." Loren rubbed the dashboard before climbing out.

Turning on the radio, he flipped to talk radio. "International model Odesi has just inked a six-figure deal to pen the un-authorized biography of Loren Smith. More details in our exclusive interview with Odesi in just a moment."

Choice words rose to his throat, but Rob put his creative visualization skills to work on how he'd kick Odesi's ass. Leaning back, he looked in the side-view mirror and spotted a black town car.

Had he not seen the car at the house earlier, he might have let it slide, but as Loren had said, there was no such thing as coincidences. Not when it came to town cars with black-tinted glass.

He dialed his cousin Hugh, who was a computer expert. His work extended far beyond Hood Investigations into the U.S. government, but he made their company a priority. He knew of Rob's situation with Loren and answered on the first ring. "We've got company stopping by later tonight. The Blacks. A new couple we met."

"How long have they been visiting?" Hugh asked, deciphering his coded language about the town car.

"Today."

"Stand by."

Rob waited for his cousin to come back. "You got any friends with you now?"

Rob knew Hugh was talking about bugs. The car had been bugged. Angry, he searched, but knew he couldn't get out and look under the bumpers because that would draw attention.

"Loren's in the store alone, and I'm waiting in the car. Just came from my doctor's appointment."

"Okay," Hugh said casually. "These are near you." The phones the Hood Team used were sophisticated computers that could also transmit video, act as scanners, as well as perform other functions. Hugh's work with the military was extensive and ongoing and allowed Hood Investigations certain exclusive advantages that they appreciated.

Rob turned the sophisticated phone slowly so Hugh could scan the car for transmitters. Who would put something inside the car instead of outside? Someone who wanted to hear what he and Loren were talking about. Someone who was arrogant enough to believe they wouldn't get caught.

"What did the doctor say about your knee?"

Knowing people were listening, Rob gave the report. "I've had a major setback. I'm on restricted duty."

Hugh shook his head and Rob saw his expression. He'd explain later. He pushed the seat back and saw a quarter-inch device barely concealed under the front dash, right in front of his denim-covered knee.

Sloppy, arrogant work.

"Feels better than it looks," he told his cousin. It was a close-range transmitter that was used to track sound and distance.

"Did the doc recommend more water aerobics or ice?" Hugh asked, telling him how to disable it.

"Both, in fact. Are we good to go?" He looked at his cousin on the sophisticated video phone.

"That's a big ten-four," Hugh said. "Hood out."

Rob grabbed the cane and went into the store, grabbing another cooler and a sixty-four-ounce bottle of water. He set it on the counter as Loren was about to pay. "You're still being bad. You know the saying, a hard head makes a soft booty or something."

"Yeah, that's it," he said drolly as several patrons gave Loren curious glances. How could Odesi have found her? He'd probably spread enough money around town for people to let him know the second Loren surfaced. Rob tried not to get angry with himself for encouraging Loren to get out of the house.

But then again, this was the time to get the man for good. Loren didn't need to be the prisoner.

In the car, he put the device in the bottom of the cooler and poured water on top of it before taking the ice and spreading that on top. He acted as if nothing was wrong, then took the ice bags to the garbage along with the transmitter. He dialed Hugh and inquired about the signal and found out it had been disabled.

Satisfied, he got back in the driver seat and waited.

Chapter 15

Rob drove through the streets of Decatur as if they were his playground. He seemed to know them so well Loren sat back and relaxed, admiring the old brick homes with lush, full lawns that would soon go dormant for the winter.

Loren could only wonder where Rob was taking her. This wasn't her part of town. Models were notorious for being in the "mix", knowing shoot and store locations and party spots, but venturing outside the city limits was reserved for one's own hometown.

She'd loved her Atlanta address because she had Marta, the rail station, just a block away, and if she absolutely needed to catch the bus, she could walk to the same corner and climb on for less than the cost of a taxi pulling away from the curb.

When she'd been a model, she'd taken that "instant access to anything she'd wanted" lifestyle for granted. Now she lived a virtual prisoner by her own choice because of fear.

She'd been wondering all day if she wanted to live that way for the rest of her life.

"What time are you going to bake?" Rob signed when Loren had gotten in the car after a last-minute purchase of a pack of gum.

"I usually start late. Ten at night or later. I used to like to bake when the neighbors were settled in for the evening."

"You don't like people?" He seemed to find the idea unfathomable.

"People are fine, but there was an expectation that I couldn't meet, and then they were always disappointed. I couldn't please everyone, so I stopped trying to please anyone."

"That's why you withdrew from society?"

"Partially. Once I stopped going out, it got easier to stay inside. After the attack, I started getting paranoid that everyone was out to get me. They wanted to hear my story." Her voice was as thick as smoke. "Everyone doesn't want to talk about everything. Everything isn't the world's right to know. I had no one to talk to because I'd cut off everyone, and Zoe, let's face it, she had her own life. Mom and Dad were dead, and psychologists always end with 'I hate to cut you off, but we're going to have to end here for today.'" She shook her head. "You could be in the middle of an absolute breakdown and they've got to go."

"That's a pretty harsh view of the world."

"Don't get me wrong, doctors have done an extraordinary job getting me through this. I'm going to have surgery to remove the scars and I'll feel better about them, but I just felt ugly. Being beautiful was all I'd ever known, and you can't talk to someone about losing your looks. They don't understand."

"That would make you vain and shallow."

"That's right. To them I still have the face and height and body. But I can't show this to anyone. I may have a degree in psychology, but it's hard to self-talk yourself off a mountain."

"Oh, baby."

"Don't feel sympathetic toward me," she said matter-of-factly. "I'm used to doing things on my own. I'm fine. Where are we going? You've got my refrigerated food on ice, and—"

"Right here."

"Where are we?"

"Downtown Decatur at the park. It's an outdoor theater. I bet you've never done this." Rob checked the mirror several times, and seemed to be satisfied. Loren looked, too, and didn't see anyone suspicious.

"What? Watched TV outside?"

Rob chuckled. "Yeah, watched TV outside. Only better."

"I have a villa in Italy, and you can sit outside and see the TV inside." Even she laughed as they got out of the car. "Okay, it's not the same."

"Get your hat and glasses, smarty."

Loren got them quickly, feeling excitement build inside of her. "What are we doing?"

"We're going on a date to a movie. Don't say no. We're here already."

"You're not supposed to be outside."

"Yes, I am. I'm supposed to be walking. You heard the doc." They got to the corner of the parking lot and a man was selling picnic baskets, small chairs and decorative blankets. Rob handed him three twenties and took a thirty-dollar basket.

"Can you help us get across the street?" Rob asked.

"Sure," the man said, happy to have such a large tip.

"That's way too much, Rob." Loren laughed as the man grinned and nearly jogged into traffic. "Give us one chair and the red print blanket."

The man did as requested and assisted them across the street.

"If you carry the basket and chair, I'll put the blanket here." Rob tried to fit it over the handle of his crutch with no success.

"I've got it. I don't mind, Rob."

His muscles bulged as he walked deftly through the crowd of couples. Women turned to look at him and several preened. Loren had to admit, Rob was one sexy, beautiful man. When she'd been working on his muscles, she'd wondered what kind of lover he'd be. The strength in his arms told her he'd be strong. The tenderness of his kiss, then the way he turned up the heat with his lips—she'd had to let the cool water of a late-morning shower vanquish her desire.

Her urges were natural, but she couldn't entertain the idea of getting more intimately involved with him. Once he saw the scars...

She heard her name several times, but she ignored the calls. She was here on a date, not to be in the spotlight.

"Is anyone sitting here?" she asked the women around her.

"You," they answered.

"Rob, this okay?"

He nodded. "Ladies," he said in greeting.

"Bruh," several women responded.

He wiggled his eyebrows at Loren and they spread their blanket and started laughing. It was tiny. Rob was at least four inches taller than Loren and the blanket was four-by-four.

"I'll go back and get another," Rob told her.

"No, let me. Your leg."

"Yo, sexy legs," someone called to Loren, "the movie is about to start."

Loren knelt and set up the chair and Rob tried to maneuver a way to get onto the ground. Several strong women got up and eased him onto the low, flat chair.

"Thanks," he said. "If you're looking for work, let's talk." Rob handed out Hood Investigations, Inc. business cards.

Two ladies handed them large blankets. "We always bring extras," a woman said.

"Thank you. This is Rob, I'm Loren," she said, extending her hand.

"Chelsea, and this is my partner, Natalie. You do know you're sitting in the unofficial gay and lesbian section."

Rob and Loren burst out laughing. "This is our first time here," Rob explained.

"We had no idea there were sections." Loren took off her hat and glasses and got up on her knees in front of Rob. As soon as people saw her, they started clapping.

"We're not gay and lesbian, but can we hang out with you and watch the movie?"

"Prove it. Prove it." The chant started and grew.

She looked down at him, her hands on his shoulders. "They want proof."

"I do, too. Tell me you trust me."

His eyes were serious and there was no compromise in them. If she said the words, she couldn't go back on them. He'd already helped her make great strides....

"I'm not going away. Odesi doesn't scare me. Say the word and we will get him," Rob told her.

"I trust you."

Gently she placed her lips against his, but what started as a simple public kiss transformed into an intimate continuation of what had begun earlier that day. Kissing him had the power to correct the tilted things inside of her. Rob's thumb was on her back, and then his hand; he was so casual, so easy in how he dealt with her. She felt herself melting, sinking into him. How long had she wanted a man like Rob in her life? A man who wanted to protect her from the bad things in her life? She opened her mouth and their tongues met. Rob didn't push because he didn't have to. He wanted her and she knew it in the way his body felt against hers. The way he leaned into her mouth, then brushed aside her hair so their lips could meet undisturbed.

Rob possessed such power but also such control, and some of the fear that had embodied her for the better part of two years was kissed away. His lips caressed hers, sending tendrils up and down her back, and she loved the old feeling like it was new again. She didn't want to pull away, but she wanted to deepen the kiss, and make up for all that she'd been missing.

The wind rustled her hair and she remembered they were

outside. She was kneeling in front of him, and with great effort, she moved her lips away, replacing them with her thumb.

"Thank you," she told him, kissing his forehead. The sky hadn't darkened and she could still see the desire in his eyes. Being outside with Rob made her feel free and safe and normal.

"You're welcome."

Sound rushed in. Loren looked around and realized people were applauding. "Shh," she told them. "We're at the movies."

Everyone laughed. She slid down Rob's chest and leaned against him, covering her legs with the borrowed blanket as they watched *Stormy Weather.*

Loren cried at the end of the movie and Rob laughed with the rest of the tough girls. Another feature played and darkness finally set in. They shared stolen kisses and caresses. When the fall wind blew, he covered her goose-bumped arms with his and made her sandwiches from their basket. She poured him wine and they chatted about their lives between features. At the end of the second feature, *Mahogany,* everyone prepared to leave and Loren folded up their basket and returned the blankets.

Walking back through the crowd, she saw Odesi's main lieutenant, Shaiku, and cold fear rippled through her. He opened his phone and started speaking as he followed her.

She hurried from the trash bins, grabbing Rob's crutches, pulling him. "Rob! Rob, we have to go. Odesi's lieutenant is here and when he saw me, he placed a call."

Rob dropped the blanket they'd brought and gently pushed Loren to the ground.

"Sit down, baby. Let me call in the team."

Loren had been used to following only her natural instinct to flee when she felt danger, but right now everything within her said to listen to Rob. She immediately obeyed.

Everyone around them sensed the change in their mood and the ladies stood and rushed over.

"Odesi Tunaotu? I've got it in for him. I worked embassy security in Washington, D.C., and because of his lies, I was terminated. Now I can't get a job in law enforcement." The woman that had been sitting next to them had been very kind, but now she looked determined and angry.

"I believe you," Loren said to her.

"What's your name?" Rob asked her, his fingers around Loren's shoulder.

"Crystal Bailey, everybody calls me Ice. I know you're Rob Hood of Hood Investigations. You gave me your card earlier. You've got a good name on the street."

"Ice, how high was your security clearance?" She told him and his eyebrow rose. "That's good. If you check out, I'm going to have something for you on Monday. Right now, I need a couple of your friends to form a barrier around Loren. I'm calling in the Trap Team, but they might not get here in time for me to get her out."

"I can get her out. I've been following what's been happening to her on TV, and I can tell you, I don't like it. Natalie is a friend and a former cop. Would you stay with Loren?"

Rob nodded and Loren silently consented.

"What does Shaiku look like?" Rob asked.

"Tall and full-bodied. Scar on his right cheek, short hair. He's probably got two or three phones. White shirt, brown pants. I didn't see his feet."

"No, that's good. Very good." Rob pushed to his feet and took his crutch.

Crystal whistled three short times and women came to see what she needed. She talked to them and they formed a tight circle, and then the row formed a wider circle and others formed an even wider circle.

Loren was impressed, though scared. Then Rob and Ice disappeared.

"Where's Rob?" Loren asked Natalie after ten minutes.

"He's probably still talking to Ice. They're planning to do exactly what they said." Natalie's phone rang and she handed it to Loren. "Hello?"

"Lakota, give your car keys to Natalie."

"Rob—"

"Trust," he said.

She inhaled. The war that waged was fierce, but she knew she couldn't get out of the park alone. The keys made an imprint in her palm, she was holding them so tight, and all Loren could think about was running. She was fast. Faster than anyone knew. She used to run five miles a day on her treadmill. But that was gone now, too.

A sob tore from her throat, and Natalie hugged her, not knowing what was wrong. Loren heard Rob's voice in her ear.

"Lakota Sky, I need you to trust me. I'm going to protect you. Now, Lakota."

Natalie rubbed Loren's arm and looked into her face. "You don't look like you trust him, but you're going to have to start believing in him sometime. He's going to a lot of trouble to help you. Why not believe in him?"

Loren removed the keys that never left her side, and handed them to Natalie, who passed them away. Loren was swept into a gigantic hug by Natalie. "You're going to be fine. You know, I've read a little about you. Your mama and daddy are gone, and you don't have siblings. Where's your best friend?"

"Out of town," Loren said into Natalie's shoulder, not meaning to be such an emotional wreck. She pulled herself away and gained control of her emotions. "She's got a boyfriend."

Natalie giggled. "Honey, you need some more friends. Tonight, I'm your second-best friend, okay?"

Loren giggled, surprised that some of her fear was slipping away with the night. "Okay. I kind of like that."

Natalie listened on her phone. "They said we're going to start moving. You're to stay bent over at the waist." A towel of questionable history was passed back. "They want you to disguise yourself as much as possible."

Loren looked at the towel. "Is this necessary?"

"Some bad people are looking for you."

"You're right." The towel was draped over her head, and she was given a pair of slip-on shoes to walk in.

Loren didn't know where she was going, but she was put into a quiet car and was on her way without Rob. This was the first time in two-and-a-half years when she'd been having a good time, and it had been ruined. Lying on the seat, she wished Rob was with her so they could rehash their evening and laugh about all the fun they'd had. Instead, a stranger was taking her home.

She was delivered to the house, and when she got there, Rob got out of a white Jeep Cherokee that had been trailing her car. He followed her up the stairs and urged her inside the dark house.

"Rob, I'm tired of being scared."

"Let me go after Odesi."

He deactivated the alarm and put his fingers to his lips. She found her defense spray and trailed him.

Rob checked every corner of the house until he was satisfied they were safe. "We're clear," he said. He pulled his phone from his waist and waited. "Hugh, assemble the team for a meeting tomorrow."

"Can't do it tomorrow, Rob. Zach and Ben are both out of town, but Mel can meet."

Rob shook his head. "I just used Trap today, and I know they both have to work tomorrow. Get both Ben and Zach here for a meeting at 0800, day after tomorrow."

Hugh nodded, and Loren was awed at the technology they used to keep each other safe. She was also grateful, but still intimidated.

"Get some rest," Hugh advised. "I've got a secondary team of off-duty cops patrolling the neighborhood tonight, so you're good for this evening."

"Thanks, Hugh. I appreciate everything." His cousin's face disappeared from the screen and he put the phone away.

Loren touched Rob's arm. "I want to talk to you about tonight, but I need to shower and get the cakes on. Afterward, okay?"

"You better believe it." Rob didn't know how the night was going to end, but he knew it would end better than the way he and Ice left Shaiku. Stuffed in the truck of his car. The Atlanta police department picked him up two minutes after they had left and had found the six guns they'd moved from his trunk to the backseat of his car.

Chapter 16

Loren sped through her shower, washing her hair and only partially drying it. Baking cakes made her feel as if she was accomplishing something, and she couldn't wait to get back to the one thing she loved to center herself after this crazy evening.

Except all of her cooking supplies were in her car!

"Rob! I can't cook. All my supplies are in my car." Hurrying out of her room, Loren walked into the kitchen and saw Ice, Natalie and a couple of other girls from the park unloading bags and putting things in the refrigerator. "Oh, my goodness. I'm so glad to see everything. And all of you."

"Your keys." Ice handed them to her.

Loren grasped them, hooking them into the waist of her shorts, and then extended her hands to all of them. "I'm so glad to see this food. Who's hungry? We've got chicken. No, I'm going to make shrimp. Everybody like shrimp? Rob," she called, "we have company."

"He let us in. He said he was going to grab a shower. We aren't going to stay," Ice said, looking shy.

"Of course you are. Come on, Natalie and Chelsea." Loren extended her hand to the woman next to Ice, who was petite and looked like she was full of energy. "I don't know your name, but you all were so nice to help me. Please let me feed you."

"I'm Maggie." Cute, Maggie was tiny next to Ice's solid and stocky build.

"Say you'll have dinner with us. It's no bother. Please?"

"I'm not going to turn down dinner," Chelsea said. "Can we help?"

"Sure. Wash up in here, and I'll get you started on the desserts."

Loren started cooking and had a brilliant idea. She hurried into the den, grabbed the remote and brought it back to the kitchen. "Rob can't figure out how to get the TV to work, just the music. Any of you want to show him?"

Ice threw up her hands. "I got this."

"I could use help with the cakes," Loren said, happy that the house was full, able to imagine what life would be like with a husband and friends. She smiled and the girls smiled back at her.

"That's my area." Natalie pulled off her short sweater and washed her hands. Loren started mixing the ingredients for the cakes, and they formed an assembly line with the baking pans. Maggie had the list of which pans got which batter, while Loren laid out extra cake pans for the firefighters' cakes. Chelsea filled the pans with batter, Natalie put them into the two separate baking ovens, while Loren got the late-evening dinner of shrimp scampi going.

Loren scoured the cabinet for appetizer foods and settled on bagged chips and salsa. "Now, what does everyone do?" Loren asked.

"I'm an actress," Maggie said, "and Ice is in law enforcement."

"I used to be a cop with a local police department, but being gay and a cop didn't go together in the small town I'm from. So I followed my second love. I'm currently an editor for an Internet magazine called *A Woman's Worth,*" Natalie said. "It's a magazine that covers stories about women who've overcome tragedies to make a better life for themselves. I've also tried my hand at broadcasting. A little color-commentating for the sports channel."

"Impressive," Loren said to both women. "What about you, Chelsea?"

"I work for the federal government, making sure you pay your taxes," Chelsea said.

The other girls booed her and Loren giggled. "Girls, that's not nice."

"What do you do?" Maggie asked Loren. The other three just stared at her. "You could be a model, you're so tall."

Loren shook her head when they were about to tell her. "I used to model a long time ago, but now I bake. I've got a culinary arts degree, so now I'm a certified chef."

Maggie eyed her. "Yeah, I can see you as a pastry chef."

Everybody hollered, laughing, even Loren.

The girls talked about everything from fashion to which dogs were the best house pets for families. Rob came downstairs and the TV was going, pots were boiling and the ladies were chatting away. He walked into the kitchen with his arms crossed, and they all looked at him. "Who the hell got the TV working?"

Everybody burst out laughing. Loren served dinner in the kitchen as the dining-room table was full of boxes. When the timers went off for the cakes, she popped up.

"I see why she stays so small. She never stops moving," Maggie said, a curvaceous size six.

"I haven't cooked since my apartment burned down two weeks ago, so this feels good. Don't they smell heavenly?" Loren spun around, the pan in her hands.

Everybody was quiet. She turned around and they all laughed at her. "What's so funny? My shorts too big? I know I've lost some weight."

"No, you're okay, but you don't have any rhythm," Natalie told her.

Loren put her hand on her hips, pretending to be offended. "Second-best friend, excuse me. I have a lot of rhythm. I have slippers on. If I had on heels I would do a better job."

"It doesn't work like that," Chelsea said, looking to the other girls for support. "You either have it or you don't. Now, you should have some if you're part black."

Loren threw up her hands, tossing her oven mitts aside and smiling. "I'm covered. My father was black."

"But it doesn't always work like that," Rob told them. "My cousin Hugh is a hundred percent black and he has no rhythm at all."

"He's a man," they all said at once, and cracked up.

"There's only one way to tell," Loren said as she iced the cakes. "We need music and I need shoes. I have a pair upstairs."

She took off through the dining room and hurried up the steps.

When she returned to the kitchen, the doorbell rang, and they all stared at one another. "Rob, are you expecting someone?" Loren asked.

He looked guilty. "I ordered food on the way home. I didn't know that you were going to feel like cooking after our night in the park."

Loren gave the remote to Ice and grabbed her defense spray. She squared her shoulders and started from the kitchen. "Find us some dance music, please. I'll go to the door with Rob."

Ice gave the remote to Chelsea and took Loren's spray. "You stay here, and I'll go to the door with Rob. I need a job."

"Good call, Ice." Rob cut a wedge of cake and put it in a disposable bowl and put a lid on it.

"What are you doing?" Loren asked.

"Nothing, woman. Put your party shoes on. I can't wait to see this."

She saw Rob's gun at his side and some of her good cheer dissipated. It returned when they came back with bags of Italian food.

Loren set all the cakes on the dining room table, and the girls helped her box and label them. They even helped her clean the kitchen. Then they danced.

Loren had never laughed so hard in her life. Ice was the worst, with a rendition of the running man that shook the house. Maggie was the best. She'd had formal training. Loren was just happy she fell in the middle.

At the end of the night she sent them home with goody bags of Italian food and cake, and promises they would get together the following weekend to cook and eat.

"You look like you had a good time." Rob took her hand as they watched the girls pull away in their cars.

"I don't think I've ever had a better time. This was the best night ever, and if you tell Zoe I said that, I'll—"

"Why are you always threatening me? You'll do what?" He spun her into him and their chests met. "Haven't I proved I've got your back? I won't ever tell your secrets."

Rob seemed to be warning her, but she wasn't afraid. That door was long closed, that woman long gone. He'd saved her too many times, protected her and now wanted to be alone with her.

"I had fun tonight. It was the best date of my life." Loren guided him from the sunroom and into the den. She slid her arms around his neck. "And because of that, I've got a special treat for you."

Chapter 17

Rob followed Loren down onto the couch and took her into his arms. Kissing her at the park, he'd had to practice restraint because they'd been in front of others, but there was no audience now. No cheers from envious onlookers or jealous spectators.

Here he was able to show her how much he appreciated their evening. He was a man, and her sweet-kiss goodness flowed from her and into him, and he claimed her mouth, loving the fullness of her lips, and the feel of her opening herself emotionally and physically to him.

"Wait, I'm not comfortable," she said. Wiggling from beneath him, she got up and turned down the music, lowered the lights, changed to a soft jazz station, then kicked off her red high heels.

"Those were the best part," he said as she walked back. He reached for her, his hands sliding up the back of her legs.

"Are you sure about that?" she asked, settling down again and making him lie so that his injured leg was on the couch. She turned on her side to face him. "I think this is better."

This time when Rob claimed her mouth, he didn't hold back the passion he'd been feeling for her. He caressed her neck and back, his yearning to have his hands on her finally realized. Their tongues tangled as his fingers twisted in her hair. Kissing her answered so many questions, filled so many spaces, settled so much of his restlessness.

She was just as passionate, her body pressed against his, her lips moist and seeking. This was what she wanted, he felt, and with that gave as much as she could handle.

Finally she pulled away and he looked at her. Her lips had turned a burnished red, and she caught her bottom lip between her teeth. There was this half-smile that tilted up her mouth and made him want to give her the keys to his kingdom.

There was a second when she looked serious, but then seduction replaced whatever thought had been in her mind and she moved his arm around her waist. "I like being closer."

Her mouth joined with his again, and she grabbed the front of his shirt, letting him know not to stop. He had no intention of doing so. This woman was so different from the woman who'd come to the house weeks ago.

He held her tight against him and left her mouth to sample her jaw and neck, and when he got to her ears she purred, deep and guttural. He could hear her laughing, and he looked into provocative green eyes. "You like that?"

She nodded, her cape of black hair falling around them. She reached up.

"Let me," he said, and pushed it out of her eyes, kissing her cheek. "I love your hair." And he turned her jaw and went to work on her other ear.

She practically stood on the toes of his good foot as he teased her lobe. She met his passion equally, keeping him close to her.

He liked that she didn't push him away, and that she smelled of cake and not perfume. She laughed when something felt good and actually purred like a contented cat whenever he pleased her. He couldn't imagine not making love to her. He wanted to so badly.

She'd built so many walls of protection around herself, he wasn't sure what he could and couldn't do. He didn't want to push her too fast and he didn't want her to change her mind. He was having his cake; he didn't mind holding it in his hands and savoring it for a while.

Her hands traveled to his neck, where she pressed gentle kisses, and when she licked him, he thought he would burst; there was a seductress inside of her.

She drove her hands beneath his light blue golf shirt. "You're very strong," she said, pulling her leg up over his hip, moving just a bit closer.

Her fingertips grazed his nipples and he bucked her a little. She grazed them again, and he bucked again. "Woman, are you trying to kill me?"

A glint of pure feminine power darkened her eyes. "You're aroused if I touch your nipples?"

Rob sat up, and she yelped at how quickly he had her in his lap and his face buried in her cleavage. He kissed the top of her breasts, but didn't try to go farther. "Does that arouse you?" he challenged.

"Yes, it does," she said, looking down at him, bald seduction in her eyes. Her arms moved around his back and she settled a little higher on his lap.

"What do you want, Lakota?"

"I want to make love to you, but this is so unlike me. I've never been this open with anyone. Not even Odesi."

"I'm not him. You can trust me."

Rob savored kissing her again.

"But?"

"I like this, too. Everything about this evening except not coming home with you. I wanted to laugh with you in the car. I wanted to hold hands. I really like your hands. I want to make love to you, but not lose this part. I liked having your friends over."

"My friends?"

He squeezed her butt until she groaned and tried to get away. "Okay! *Our* friends over. I've never had girlfriends. Ever."

They both found that funny.

"I'm glad you told me," he said, kissing her neck until she drew her nails up and down his back in crazy circles. She spoke in a language he didn't understand.

"What are you saying?" he asked her.

"That feels good. Do that again."

"So you *do* want me!"

Loren laughed in her throat. "Yes, Rob. But it's a process."

"You like the idea of us being more than friends?" He threw it out there, hoping their goals were the same. She'd said no man would ever touch her, but she'd professed her trust and had put her words into action. She was trusting him now.

"I think we're more than that now, but I don't want to jump into anything when I'm so vulnerable."

"Baby, you're strong," he said sincerely. "Believe it."

Loren looked like she was becoming stronger every time he encouraged her. He pushed her beautiful hair back so he could see her eyes fully. "You look better. Happier and more relaxed. How would you categorize us?"

"Colleagues?" she suggested.

"Do you do this with all your colleagues?" he asked, alternately squeezing her butt cheeks.

Loren burst out laughing and kicked. She twisted his nipples to make him stop, but he wasn't deterred. "No! I don't," she giggled, unable to stop the slide of her shorts from practically becoming a thong.

Burying his face in her hair and neck, he inhaled. "Oh, my, girl, don't hurt me."

She caressed his face with her nose. "Rob, we are what we are."

"I need a clear definition. I don't want you using me for my body." He leaned up and reached the ornate chest that was full of blankets. He chose a thick chenille blanket and brought her closer to him, one arm around her back, the other pulling her leg over his. "So, no sex tonight? Is that what you're saying?"

She laughed. "No, just for a little while." He accepted her kisses and her gorgeous smile, and the plea she made with her eyes. He nearly couldn't resist her.

"You want to make out with me and leave me for days? You're a mean, cruel woman. What am I supposed to do? What can I touch? Tell me so I know the hot zones."

"Hot zones?" she asked, breathing on his neck.

Rob cradled her and pushed his nose into her neck, while he ran his hand from her shoulder down her breasts to her hip, around to her butt, to the back of her thigh. He urged her leg up, moved his between her legs and applied just enough pressure to give her something to think about. In the dimmed light he knew she'd gotten his message.

Her eyes closed slowly, and she was breathing as if she'd just come in from a brisk walk.

"I know that you want to make love to me. But something is holding you back. I'm going to respect you, but, baby, this is not going to be easy for me, and that means I'm not going to make it easy for you."

"Rob—"

"Have I ever told you I love your accent?"

She giggled as he kissed the tops of her breasts again. "Yes, you have," she said graciously. "Rob?"

She pointed to her breasts. "No touching here and here," she said, and then pointed between her legs and then her butt. "Here."

"No. Flag on the play." He tossed a decorative pillow from the couch to the floor and grabbed her bottom. "I have to be able to touch your ass, Lakota."

"Why, Rob?" She couldn't stop laughing as he held her bottom and shook her whole body.

"Because it's there. When you're cooking, I see your eyes first and then your ass. I'm an ass man." He caressed it now, his hands possessing it. "These shorts?" He sighed and kissed her forehead, then her mouth, in a long lingering kiss that made him so hard he could nail a wall in place. "See, your ass likes me."

Loren scooted up a bit and their bodies molded better. "My whole body likes you. But my body isn't in charge. My brain is."

"You should listen to your body, baby. But—" he breathed hard "—no pressure. These are negotiations. I should be given one cheek a day or at least alternating cheeks."

"Now, that's silly." Her hair was everywhere and her green eyes were happy.

"No, it's not. This is a compromise. If I can't have both, I need just one. Just lean against me. I want to show you the benefits of a good ass rub. Come right here."

"Rob, no. You're so kinky." He had her right where he wanted her, because even though she was protesting with her mouth, she wasn't pulling away.

"Is it kinky to feel good?"

"No," she said reluctantly.

"Do you feel good? And I want you to think for a full minute before you answer. Before you answer, think about how you've felt all year and how you feel right now."

She leaned against him and didn't move.

He kneaded her bottom and massaged, pressing her into him.

"Rob, this isn't fair," she said breathlessly.

"Shh. The minute isn't up."

His hands moved to her thighs and then slowly up over the

rise of her bottom to her back. "I do feel good, but I feel guilty."

"Why?"

"We just met."

"No, we didn't," Rob said easily, kissing her neck and collarbone.

"We met—" her head fell back, granting him access.

"Last year at my house. Zoe asked you to cook for my family while we worked on her case. I thought you were gorgeous. I wanted to know you then. That was technically the first time or I wouldn't have you on this couch."

She didn't want to laugh, but her chest shook against his, anyway.

She planted a tiny kiss on his chin. "Aah," she said, and he wanted to hear it again. He kept caressing her bottom.

He guided her core against his desire. Her eyes narrowed and her hands braced the couch beside his head.

Rob moved her hips in tandem with his. Faster he brought her against him, pressing her harder into him as he willed her pleasure to come. She no longer fought as he felt her climax building, her eyes barely open, her bottom lip caught between her teeth, her breasts straining against the fabric of her clothing.

He wanted to be inside her so badly. Knowing he couldn't, he made her feel him, holding her close, his sex to hers, her mouth wide-open, her gasps wearing at his resistance to follow her rules.

"Rob, please, yes." Loren sought release and her hands were all over his face, his chest and finally at his neck.

"Oh" tore from her powerfully as she came, her whole body shaking, her hair drowning him in black silk. Her mouth came down on his, her tongue hungry for his. He grabbed her ass hard and came against her. Their bodies shook, and he heard himself calling her name until the tingles subsided. Loren didn't say anything, but she didn't pull away, either.

They lay together for a long time. Slow jazz played from the darkened TV, lightened occasionally when the song changed. Rob could have stayed that way all night, when he felt her stir. He realized his good leg was wrapped around hers and the blanket was entangled between them.

"One request?" he asked.

Her eyelashes shielded her trepidation. "What is it?"

"For my birthday present, I want you to dance for me."

"No."

"Not the dance you did for that designer. That dance you did tonight with the girls. You all were ridiculous."

She rolled her eyes. "I'll think about it."

"Kiss me, Lakota."

Time and laughter slipped away. The tentative threads of their relationship wove together. He loved the gentleness of her touch, and he wanted her to know his touch would never harm her.

"I'm so glad to have met you, Rob," Lakota whispered. "I don't know what else to say." Lacing her fingers with his, she brought his hand to her abdomen. "This is important, you see. I still can't take my clothes off."

He held his breath and closed his eyes.

He'd gone through something like this when he'd found out his niece couldn't hear anymore. For three days he'd intentionally not spoken and worn earplugs so he'd be able to understand her world. Still, at the end of the weekend, he was left frustrated and angry at how insensitive people were.

It was hard to erase fear.

Her hand was shaking and he let her guide his under her top.

He touched the skin. The flesh was healed, but it felt like rope or a twisted wrapper. And it was hard. Rob squinted, trying to imagine in his mind's eye what he was feeling. He pulled her top up to look and she flew off the couch.

"No!"

Her panic shocked him, and he tried to sit up and calm her down. "I'm sorry. I didn't mean to do that. Come back, Loren."

"No, I'm tired. I'm going to bed." Running, she stumbled over her shoes but caught herself, and when she got to her bedroom, she slammed the door and locked it.

Rob's head fell back and he shook it. He went to her door and put the shoes outside.

"Loren, I'm sorry."

"It's okay. I'm just going to go to bed. I have to get up early tomorrow, anyway, and get my stuff out of my apartment. So... good night."

"Okay." He waited, his head on the doorjamb. "Good night."

He'd really messed that up, but he wasn't taking all the blame. Odesi had physically harmed her and he was going to pay. In Hood cash.

Chapter 18

Loren clawed at her throat. She was being choked to death and she awoke to find her hair wound around her neck.

She sat up, sweeping the hair back in a way that reminded her so much of her mother. An intense need to connect with family overcame her, and she called Zoe. "Where are you?"

"Cabo San Lucas. How are things at home?"

Come home. Loren wiped tears from her eyes, wishing her best friend was minutes away. She drew her knees up and leaned her chin on her legs. "I thought you were home."

"We were, but we decided to come down here for four days. Our vacation is over soon. Rob's called an executive meeting so Ben's going to be there."

"I know. There was an incident in the park. I got up last night to get something for my headache, and I overheard Rob asking Hugh to assemble the entire team for a meeting," Loren said, guilt filling her. "He also said he viewed the information on the flash drive I gave to him."

"Ben was on the phone part of the night with Rob, but it seems that they worked out the problem. Honey, I've got to run. I'll call you later today. Water my plants, please."

"Of course," Loren said quickly. "I'll do it now. Love you."

"Love you, too. Bye."

What could Rob have wanted with Ben in the middle of the night? Well, they *were* twins, she reasoned. The conversation could have been about anything. Probably about how she had lost it last night. He probably thought she was broken inside and not worth the effort. He was the first man who'd shown genuine interest and affection for her, the first who'd stayed around long enough to suffer through her intense rejection process, and now he was calling in his brother to drag him out alive.

Poor thing. And she'd promised to be nice.

Loren looked at the clock. Five-thirty. She had arrived here this time nearly three weeks ago. Nobody was up but her and the birds. She might as well clean the house. She changed from pajamas to shorts in response to the heat of the morning, watered the plants first, then cleaned the entire lower level of the house before seven-thirty.

Planning to leave before eight-thirty, she showered and dressed and was fixing breakfast when she heard Rob stumble and fall down the stairs.

Rob had done a good job of catching himself with one hand on the banister, but he couldn't believe he was on his butt, his back facing the stairs, about to tumble to his death.

In seconds Loren was behind him. "What are you doing?"

She sounded terrified.

"I'm going to lean against you," she told him, grabbing the railing and the banister, pushing her torso against his back. "I'll stabilize you with my body. Then turn into me. Turn your bottom around on the stairs, okay?"

"Okay. Give me a little space. I don't want to knock you down, too." He was, after all, still a man.

"I'm strong. I won't fall and I won't let you fall," she said, leaning around to look at him. "Please, Rob, let me help you."

Even though her words were meant to reassure him, he wouldn't let go of the banister. "If we both go down these stairs, it's your fault."

She put her hand on his shoulder. "Blame me for your clumsiness," she teased.

She slipped her hand between his knees, something she wouldn't have done last night, and guided his right leg around. He let the railing go in degrees. The muscles quivered in his calf and back and she held his body weight through her torso and thighs. "You're doing good, sweetheart. Just a little more. A little bit more."

As soon as he was around far enough, Rob lowered his foot and scooted back on the top step. Then he dropped his head into his hands and scrubbed his face. Loren stepped up and rubbed his head. "Are you okay? Do you want some water?"

"I've had enough water for today, thanks." He gestured toward the floor.

The water he'd slipped in had come from a plant she'd watered. It had leaked out of the planter onto the marble floor, and when he'd left his room, disaster, he'd explained.

"I don't know what to say. I'm so sorry. How are you feeling? Are you hurt seriously anywhere? Should I call Dr. Dillard?"

She touched him then, his legs, his thigh, his arms, and when she touched his wrist it was warm. "Rob, you okay?"

"I'm a little banged up, but I'm fine." He stopped her hands. "Really."

He moved to stand and she got in front of him. "Whoa, cowboy. Where're you going?"

Embarrassed, he wanted to take the last five minutes away. "To the den."

"This is your new way of going down the stairs." She sat down and scooted down on her butt. "No more walking until we know what we're dealing with."

He would never admit that it made better sense. That following the doctor's instructions made sense and staying in the lower bedroom made sense. "Who made you the boss?"

"You did when you nearly killed yourself. Now, come on."

His pride stung, but he could hardly deny her. At the bottom, she handed him the fallen crutches.

"You didn't have to come down the stairs like that, too," he told her as she ushered him into the room and got him settled on the sofa. She sat on the divan and helped him get his knee into a comfortable position. Her hands on his leg reminded him of the strides they'd made yesterday and how it ended. Her running away, her arms clutched over her stomach, him behind, telling her it was okay.

"I know, but I feel bad. Relax a minute and I'll be right back. Anything hurt?" she asked from the kitchen.

"Not more than anything else."

"Not your sprained wrist?" she said, sexy and smooth over his head.

He opened his eyes and met green water in the depths of her eyes. "Yes, Dr. know-it-all. My wrist hurts, but it always does after I fall down a staircase."

Her eyebrow slid up, and had he been more agile, and she not scared of him, he'd have chased her down and made love to her right then.

"I think someone needs an attitude adjustment."

Rob gritted his teeth against the pain in his lower back. But that wasn't the only place on his body that needed attention. "I know you're not talking, Lakota Sky Thunderhawk, the queen of attitudes."

She returned with ice for his knee and wrist and a cup of coffee. Rob accepted her offerings and she took her place on the divan, looking worse than she had yesterday.

"What's wrong with you?" he asked. "What happened last night?"

"I wanted you to touch the scars, not look at them. They're

hideous. I look at them because they remind me of what he did to me. But I never let anyone else see them."

"Do you still want him, love him?"

"No!"

Angrily, she jumped up and went off. She muttered in her native language. Fury and frustration burst out of her in a great well of emotion. He saw the fire that had been dormant was now awakened and that soon her spirit would fully be restored. When Loren was close enough to him, he grabbed her with his uninjured hand and pulled her to him. In a second she was on her knees on the sofa facing him.

"Stop," he told her.

Her mouth closed yet her heart raced. He let two minutes pass. "Say it all again in English. You were speaking a little Lakota and some Italian, although *bastard* is a universal word."

"No, most of it was vile." She swiped an angry tear away.

"Why are you angry with me?"

"I'm not angry with you. I like you, although you wouldn't know that. I just don't want you to see them," she whispered. Her eyes welled with tears.

"Why? Tell me, Lakota."

"I'm vulnerable to your thoughts and your feelings. You have the power to hurt me."

"You think I'm not vulnerable? Your knees are an inch away from my nuts." Her smile was quick, fleeting. "Seriously, there are a lot of reasons you're hiding these scars. Tell me."

"I think they're ugly. They make me ugly." She covered her eyes. "That's why. I don't feel pretty anymore, and I traded on my looks for money for years. I was shallow and vain and self-indulgent. And now that I can't model anymore, I have to find something else to do with my life. I stopped going out because I hoped the world would forget me."

Now he understood. In her own eyes, she wasn't pretty.

"Lakota, the world never forgets something great. You're gorgeous, but eventually all beauty fades. You've said that yourself. Your career would have ended eventually, right? The scars don't matter. It's how you deal with them that others will learn from."

"I know. But I've lived off this body forever. I've heard I was beautiful from the time I could understand language. These past two years I've reprogrammed my brain. I'm not beautiful anymore. But you keep saying that I am, and if you see them, you might change your mind and hurt me terribly."

He kept a firm grip on her. "I'm not a liar."

"I know. When you tried to look at them, I thought it would change the way you saw me and I got so scared I ran like a child. I'm so sorry. That was so childish."

"Okay. It's okay, baby. Please stop crying."

She swept her hair behind her ears, her eyes seeking reassurance before she closed them.

"What if I told you I had a big secret?" He knew it was risky, but he had to tell someone.

"What is it?"

He began slowly. "I was investigating Gunther Madison, a man who had cheated his partners out of their share of the business and had left with the money. Our job was to find Gunther, but more important, get the money back. We did our jobs. But we Hoods have a philosophy. If we find out you've done the other party wrong, with malicious intent, you will pay the Hood tax."

"What's that?" she asked, sitting back.

"The person will pay ten times what he owes."

"That's a lot." She began to massage his arm in gentle strokes, her lashes wet.

"It's a matter of honor. We don't deal in petty crimes. We deal in serious wrongdoings. Well, good ol' Gunther decided he was going to ram me with his car, only I wasn't in a car at the time."

"You got hit by a car?"

"No, I got out of the way in time, but my knee was still going the other way. Ben recovered Gunther and I got a new knee for his trouble. His partners got their money back, and there's a playground at a school in Augusta that has a generous, anonymous benefactor."

"You?"

Rob shook his head. "Gunther."

She chuckled. "That's wonderful. Is this what you do all the time? How do you get away with that?"

"His partners thought it more prudent to give the money to the city than have us Hoods deal with it."

"Your knee will get better. You'll be back to your old self."

"My secret is that my old self is a memory. I keep feeling like I'm getting too old for this business. Then what will I do?"

She looked almost innocent. "Rob, you're smart. You could be a judge like we talked about. You executed that whole plan for me the other day from the couch. You're the brains behind the operation. Not a lot of people could have pulled that off. You have to look at work differently."

"Like you?"

She looked unsure. "Perhaps. You won't have to pursue a whole new profession if this is what you love. Just approach it from a different standpoint. You recruited Ice last night just from meeting her."

"You're so full of answers for me, but for yourself you don't see the forest for the trees."

"People are blind to their own talents and faults. I'm no different. I'm learning. I'm curious, too. I'd like to know how you'd get Odesi?"

"I can't tell you."

"Why not?"

"Because if you were ever to testify, I'd want you to tell the truth. You don't know anything."

"If you were to go after him, would he know that I was involved?"

"Not if you don't want him to."

'Would he go to jail?"

"That would be left to the justice system, but we'd get a confession."

"You would?"

Rob nodded. "A confession makes it easier for him to go to jail for a long time."

"The justice system isn't a friend to Native Americans. It's rarely worked in our favor. I don't know, Rob."

"That won't be the case this time."

"You sound very sure of yourself. He's gotten away with being a criminal for a long time, and he has diplomatic immunity."

"No, he doesn't. His father does, but that doesn't give him an exemption card from punishment."

"There have been attempts to prosecute him, but he is his father's only son. The ambassador has paid off a lot of people for his son to remain free in the hopes that he'd straighten out and one day follow in his footsteps. I told you before attempts had been made to get him, but no woman has been successful in prosecuting him. Knowing that, I won't even attempt it, Rob."

"Let us handle it," Rob said.

He saw the flicker of gratitude a few seconds before she got closer to him. Her hands were holding his and her lips were a breath away. Then she kissed him.

Rob thought the couch moved, but it was only Lakota, leaning up and into him, wrapping her arms around him as she teased his lips with her tongue.

He didn't want to expect too much or ask for too much, but

he couldn't start here again. Dawning lit her eyes. "I want to make up with you."

"Why?"

"I'm ready now." She removed the sweater she'd been wearing that looked too old for her. "I wish it was last night again, and dark." She seemed so nervous, but he wouldn't make it easy for her.

He shook his head. "I don't." She had on a thin-strapped top that fit her body, but not too tightly. "You shouldn't be ashamed of your body. Even with the scars you're gorgeous."

"You haven't seen them."

"They won't change my mind about you."

She took his hand and kissed his fingertips. He'd never thought of his hand as large, but compared to her torso it looked huge. Slowly she loosened the top from her skin and slid his hand beneath it.

Rob knew he wouldn't make any mistakes this time. He made sure his touch was gentle, but he wanted her to know that nothing would scare him away. He fixed his gaze on hers and touched her.

"What does it feel like?" she asked him.

"Like I'm about to be the luckiest man in the whole world."

Chapter 19

The scar felt like a caterpillar except it was corded and hard. "He meant those to be fatal, the doctor said."

"Does it still hurt?" he asked, hurting for her.

"This is going to sound as if I'm an old lady, but I can tell when it's going to rain. Sometimes it itches."

He smiled at her. "My knee."

"We're not in our twenties and thirties having this discussion, are we?" she asked.

"Yes, baby. Where else?"

"Right here." She guided his hand to her rib cage and he felt the long scar.

Rob closed his eyes. "Where else, baby?"

"Here," she said, unzipping the top of her shorts. Their gazes clashed as he felt her smooth skin first, then the contrasting scar.

"Will that affect your ability to have—"

"No, but I don't think I'll ever have children."

"Why?"

She just shook her head, the words unable to form. "Not in my cards."

He ran his thumb over the scar and couldn't imagine all she'd endured. Odesi had not meant to harm her, but to kill her. And when he hadn't, he'd been happy knowing he'd taken away the one thing she'd loved, and that was modeling. Now he had a platform, and he'd been on talk shows since the announcement of Loren's death, telling of how she'd been crazy the days before her "incident." Now that she was alive, he'd stated that she'd planned the fire to get more attention. He couldn't explain why she hadn't refuted any of his ridiculous accusations.

Rob surmised that all of the attention Odesi was generating was to revive his faded modeling career, but the bug in the car and the man at the movies last night were an effort to find Loren and put an end to what he had started in Monaco.

Rob vowed to catch Odesi and take him down.

He gazed at the woman in his arms. "Did he hurt your breasts?"

She shook her head.

"Will you take these off for me?" Rob only fingered the spaghetti straps on her top but didn't move them. This had to be her decision.

She nodded, and as he held her waist, she brought her arms through the straps, her hands coming to rest on his shoulders. Her touch was gentle, caressing, and he kissed her palm.

There was passion inside of her and he wanted to awaken it. He'd experienced it when she was angry. Seen it when she'd dumped the entire silverware drawer on the floor, leaving him in the kitchen with the remnants of her helpless fury. He'd had a time cleaning that up.

But even as he held her in his hands, she looked like she could change her mind at any second.

"You sure you don't want to take it all the way off?"

"Not yet."

"Give them to me," he said. She pulled the top lower, exposing two of the most beautiful brown-tipped breasts he'd ever seen.

She took his left hand and kissed the back of it before placing it over her breast. Rob gazed into her eyes and caressed the beautiful mound, loving the feel of her skin. The swell of womanliness birthed against the center of his palm, and he felt as if he'd been pierced, as the tip grew into a knot.

He carried the weight of it in his other hand and sank his face into the center of her chest and inhaled, her hair blessing him in strokes across his face and neck. Her nails scratched his back enough to make him aware, but not enough to distract, and all his senses were alert as he breathed in the scent and taste and touch of Lakota.

He breathed in again and heard the moan of longing start low in her belly. A very gentle sound that he wanted to become breathless. She hadn't been touched by another person in years, and he was honored that she'd chosen him. She was so soft. Softer than the Ultrasuede they were sitting on. Softer than cotton. Softer than the word *beautiful*.

He kissed her mouth and cheek, and then brought her to him and closed his lips over her breast. She even tasted beautiful.

He exhaled. She did, too.

"Yes." The word seemed to come out of her from a distant place on a slow, low moan. She pressed down on his shoulders, arching, straining for him to take more of her. Her nipple bloomed on his tongue and she responded by pulling him closer.

Each time he moved to the other breast her head fell forward against his and she kissed him, her hand on top of his hand as if she were directing him to the more under-served breast.

Her nails were short, but she tantalized him by raking up his arms and back.

He took her to the couch with him, unable to satisfy himself by not having her beside him. She inched closer and he moved back and, careful of his slightly aching wrist, pulled his shirt over his head. He had to feel her against him, he had to.

Loren sensed his need to and helped him, and even before his shirt was completely off she was against him, her hair making him feel as if he was being stroked by a bolt of cake-scented silk fabric. She suckled his nipple and he lurched up off the couch, sending them both into a fit of laughter. "It's been a long time."

"For me, too," she said, reaching for him.

"I didn't mean to laugh," he explained, caressing her head, then bringing her back down with him.

"You didn't hurt my feelings too badly."

"You wouldn't fix your mouth, you faker," he chastised, looking into her eyes as he touched her belly scar. "I'm going to kiss your scar, Lakota."

"Rob, you don't have to," she said, her smile wavering. She leaned up on her elbows.

"I'm already touching it and I haven't run for the door. In fact, my eyes will be closed when I do kiss it."

"Really? Why do you want to?"

"Because you think it's something terrible and I don't. I'm closing my eyes."

"Wait!" She lay back down. "I don't want to see this." He took her by the butt and squeezed, yanking her denim shorts half off. "Rob!" She started kicking and laughing and made a halfhearted attempt to get them back up, but her effort was no match for his. "You're only supposed to be touching one cheek at a time."

"You're breaking my heart. I thought you forgot."

With that he lifted her, cheek in one hand, and kissed her scar. The scar was thin and looked like a long centipede, nothing for her to be ashamed of, but everything to a woman who had made her living on her looks.

He'd promised he wouldn't look until she was ready for him to see her scars, and he would keep his word, so without using his eyes, he let his tongue guide him down the length of the thin long scar all the way to the hardened tip.

Loren's voice was naturally husky, but it sounded like rustling fall leaves with each breath she took, and when she caressed his head and sighed with an "Oh," he lifted her just a little higher and let his tongue demonstrate how much he wanted her.

Then he simply kissed it. For all of her hurt and all of her pain, he wanted to replace bad with good. He wanted to let her know there was so much better in this room than she'd ever had in her entire life.

His desire for her mounted, and when she relaxed and let go of the couch, he claimed her breasts, her hands reaching for him.

Careful of his leg, Rob took her by the thighs and brought her on top of him. At this moment, he couldn't imagine sleeping alone again.

Her eyes effused passion and she linked hands with him. One by one she licked all of his fingers, setting his body on a slow boil. Then she guided his hand to her center, and when he touched her, she arched and inhaled. Everything stopped, for just a second.

Fiery green eyes met his. "More."

Rob sat up and claimed her breasts, swinging around so that his leg was supported by the divan and her body was spread, granting his access. There was so much that he wanted from her, wanted *for* her, and he was going to give it to her right now. "Come for me."

"No," she said.

He claimed her mouth, ravishing her lush lips, sucking the bottom one that he hadn't been able to stop dreaming about. He'd dreamed of it everywhere on him.

He brought her against the tautness of his sex and rocked her. His mouth touched hers and he drove his fingers through her hair. "I dreamed of you, making love to you, of you making love to me, and you came. Just like you did yesterday."

"Oh, did I?"

"Yes, baby. Come for me."

His thumb worked her clit, and she moved against him, his mouth taking her breast earnestly. She'd kneeled up and he held her, even as she pushed against his hand, moaning to him in Lakota. Her flood of juices warmed his hand. He understood her hair all over his face and her nails scratching his arm as she descended, and he knew what her kisses meant when she told him how beautiful her climax was.

Before he knew it, Rob was on his back and she was lying full length on top of him.

"What will make you come?" Rob asked sexily.

"Don't play games with me." Loren laughed, while she pinched his pecs.

"Ow, woman!" He grabbed just one cheek of her butt and pressed her against him. "You, right there, is a good start. If you tell me how great our sex life is going to be, I'll die happy."

"It's going to be beautiful. We're going to make love under the stars and every time will be filled with raw passion. I'm going to devour you until you don't want anyone else."

Rob took both cheeks in his hands and pressed her against him. She was irresistible: her green eyes, the cape of her hair. As she lay wrapped in his arms, she beckoned him with "Come, baby." And he did.

Seconds turned to minutes and they lay there. Rob wanted to ask her if she meant what she'd said. Wanted to know if her words had a shred of truth to them, but his cell phone rang.

The phone had been discarded on the floor long ago, so Rob had to abandon holding her to reach for it, but Loren got to it first and gave it to him. "Hello?" he said gruffly.

"This is Chef Phillipe for Loren. Is she available?"

Rob smiled up at her. "It's for you. Chef Phillipe."

"I don't know a Chef Phillipe."

"Trust me, this is a call you want to take. He's a friend, I sent him a sample of your work."

Loren took the phone. "Hello?"

"Loren, thank you. Thank you. The cake you sent with my deliveryman last night was delectable. I apologize for not getting back to you last evening, but the time got away from me, and so I am calling you now."

"You're welcome." Rob sucked her nipples while she talked. "Aah, um. I'm so pleased you liked it. I'd be happy to send a whole cake anytime."

"Excellent. Say six cakes a night to start. I would have to know your fee. I can't go higher than thirty dollars a cake."

"You're kidding, right?" She looked as if she couldn't believe the chef was offering to pay her. "Six cakes a night?"

Rob laid her down, sliding his palm over her fully blossomed nipple. "How much?" he signed, and she told him. Rob lifted his thumb over his head, telling her to go higher.

"Okay, Loren. Fifty dollars. But in lemon and white."

Her hand rested on the back of his head as he tugged her nipple between his teeth. "Yes." She sighed. "That's good, I mean, closer to the ballpark, but I'm going to have to get back to you on that, Chef."

"Sixty dollars, Loren."

Rob shook his head no as Loren nodded. She squint her eyes in protest at Rob.

"Seventy-five, your delivery guy picks them up, and you've got a deal, Chef."

"You drive a hard bargain, but it's a deal. What is your last name, Loren?"

She replied softly, "Smith."

"Oh, my sweet heaven. *The* Loren Smith? What is your agent's name?"

She simply held Rob's head in place and he loved it. "Dionne Kelly. Why?"

"I want to talk to her. I want to tell her some of my ideas. We will do some great business!"

"Chef Phillipe," she managed to say, but her mouth was already pressed against Rob's.

Rob took the phone from her. "*You* got her cheap, Phillipe," Rob said to his good friend. "She's got another call. She'll call you back later."

"Rob, you are a sly one not telling me it is the great Loren Smith I am working with," Phillipe chastised gently. "But I will forgive you because her work is outstanding. I will take care of this," he said happily. "And you, my friend, take care of her."

"I will. Goodbye, Phillipe," Rob said kindly.

Rob clicked the off button and let her climb onto him. He was going to take his punishment like a man.

"I should be so angry with you," Loren told him, her center connecting with snug precision with his.

"Why? And it's hard to take you seriously when your lovely breasts are staring at me."

Loren covered them with her arms. "You went behind my back and solicited work for me."

"No, I didn't. Like I said. I sent a friend a sample of your work. There's a difference."

He bent his left leg and enjoyed the view of her hair, her smile, the twinkle in her eyes, her breasts, her confidence and her freedom.

Rob cupped her neck and she came to him. "Thank you so much, Rob. What am I going to do with you?" She nuzzled him. "What time is it?"

"Nine."

Loren disentangled herself and got up. "We have to go. I have to get my things out of my apartment. Come on. We can lie around later."

"Do you promise?"

"Isn't tomorrow your birthday?"

Rob snagged Lakota and brought her back to him. Deliberately, he kissed her scar, then fastened and zipped her shorts.

"That was the hardest thing I've had to do in a long time."

She offered both hands to pull him up. "Maybe we can play when we get home."

"You've got yourself a deal."

As soon as they walked out of the house, Loren reached for Rob's hand. "Something doesn't feel right."

For the third week in September, the street was totally quiet, no squirrels bustling around. The men who usually stood on driveways or mowed lawns before the day's heat set in were no-where around, and the morning walkers seemed to have chosen different routes. It was eerily quiet.

"It's a beautiful September day," he signed. "Let's just enjoy it."

He knew exactly what she meant. That's why he was carrying both guns.

Chapter 20

Loren's reaction to being in her apartment complex was as complicated as she was. She looked upon it with loving eyes, and Rob was surprised.

"Those flowers were planted just this spring. They bloomed so beautifully and I thought the children would have picked them all, but they didn't."

"Did you plant any?"

A quick toss of her head gave him his answer. "I watched from the deck and gave the hundred dollars to buy the flowers. Oh. The Men and a Truck company is already here. I doubt I have enough stuff for six men."

"Well, if they're moving stuff from the storage unit and the apartment, the work will go faster with that many men."

"Hadn't thought of that." Loren pulled her hair into a ponytail. "We can park in either of the two spaces here. These are mine."

"What did the insurance company say?"

"They're paying my unit off. I can rebuild and take temporary housing on this property. My problem is that I still don't know what caused the fire. Once I know, I'll decide what to do."

A small crowd had gathered, along with some paparazzi.

"You see the photographers," he warned.

"I do. I saw Xan, too. I suspect Mel is here somewhere?"

"You're becoming quite the observant agent," he told her.

"I try to pay attention. It's saved my life," she said softly.

Rob squeezed her hand, and instead of pulling away, she held it for a few seconds.

An eager old woman waved as they stopped, but she was ordered back by police. She tried to explain and then walked off, glancing over her shoulder at Loren.

"Who's that?" Rob asked.

"I don't know her name, but she gave me ten dollars the night of the fire. I would like to give it back."

Rob put his arm around her shoulders. "I knew there was a heart in there, tin woman."

"Shut up before I take your knee out."

"Always the knee with you."

Loren approached the officer and showed her license. "I was told I could get my things out of my apartment and my storage unit."

The officer spoke into his radio. "Inspector Clark? Ms. Smith is on the premises with… Sir, your name?"

"Rob Hood of Hood Investigations." Rob spoke loud enough so nothing would have to be repeated.

"Send them in."

Loren walked ahead of Rob, but never let go of his hand. She'd gotten outside of Zoe's house, all right, but wading through the photographers here at her apartment was a little more difficult. He felt her shaking.

They headed inside what must have been a very nice, luxurious place. But no one would have known it. There wasn't anything inside. All of the furniture had been removed.

"Rob, where's my stuff?" she asked, sounding astonished.

"Lieutenant?" Rob turned, expecting a full explanation for the empty living room. Looking into the kitchen, he saw that even the refrigerator was gone.

"When we left the furniture was here. Someone must have stolen it, Ms. Smith."

"How's that possible?" Loren asked, running to where a cabinet must have stood. "My mother and father's pictures were right here. The photo albums were in the case I had built right here. It weighted fifty pounds. You can't just walk out and nobody not see anything."

"Ms. Smith, I'm sorry. I called the police and they're on the way. As soon as I arrived and saw what happened, I placed the call."

The lieutenant approached Rob. "The night we came in here there was fire in the walls. It's been determined her unit had too much power coming to it. The power overheated the breakers."

"Aren't they supposed to automatically shut down?" Loren asked, looking as if she wanted to cry. "That's what they said when they installed the stove and warmer ovens."

"Yes, but they failed. It was a case of human error. I'm sorry. The investigator is out back and will have a report when he comes inside. I've gotta go downstairs and explain to the couple below."

Rob stopped him. "Were their belongings stolen, too?"

"No. But the fire moved up the walls, and while we got here in time to get to the fire, they had extensive water damage and lost everything."

"Please express our sorrow," Rob said.

The lieutenant nodded. "You have five minutes up here."

Rob looked for Loren in the back of the spacious apartment. He'd imagined her living space as being wide-open and he was right. He found her in the bathroom, sitting on the side of the tub, a tube cap in her hand.

"They took my chairs. They even took my soap."

"It's all replaceable, darling." The whole thing gave him an eerie feeling.

"Not the pictures of my parents. That's all I really cared

about." She walked through every room, checking the closets, and found nothing.

Leaving the apartment, she walked with her hands in her pockets, her head down. Loren descended three levels and arrived at her unit in the basement, and Rob saw that it was empty, too. She then moved to the next one, number 208. "This one is mine."

Rob pushed off the wall. "Not 207?"

"No. When I moved in it was still full of someone's junk so they gave me 208 and whoever lived in 208 got mine, 207."

"Theirs is empty."

She shrugged as she used her key to open the lock. "Mine isn't." Her face broke into a sad smile. "This is cast-off stuff, but maybe there's a photo of Mom and Dad in here. Maybe I can have it restored."

Rob touched her shoulder. "Let's take the photo albums and pictures back to the house and let the storage guys put this on the truck."

She squeezed his hand. "Okay, I'll go get the guys."

He offered her his handkerchief. "Wipe your tears."

Surprised, she dried her face. "I really appreciate—"

"Don't." Rob bumped her chin. "Hurry up so tomorrow can get here faster."

The six moving men made short work of the boxes and furniture in the storage unit, leaving it a dusty shell within an hour.

Loren hovered, hoping the pictures would be of her parents. She finally emerged from the building to a gray sky and a somber mood. She'd found no pictures of her parents and she wanted to cry, but Rob saw her stubborn streak emerge as she lowered the bill on her hat and put on her glasses. That meant she was inaccessible. The little old lady approached this time and wouldn't be held back by the cop.

"Ms. Loren, I never knew your name before, but you always waved."

Loren's smile was patient. "I'm sorry for not being nicer. I was having a difficult time. I wanted to thank you for your generosity the night of the fire. You gave me money and no one was kinder to me than you." Loren pressed a hundred dollar bill into the old woman's hands.

"Well, thank you. That's really nice, and I can't wait to tell everybody at church," the woman said. "I'm Nera. I live a building over and I saw some men come and go in the middle of the night from your house."

Rob and Loren stood straighter. "When was this?" Rob asked.

"Oh, right after the fire. Two weeks ago. We had revival at my church, and you're supposed to stay up all night and pray. Well, I got tired and decided to come home at about one in the morning. I was parking and I saw them moving your bed out, quiet as mice."

"Really?" Loren said, slightly breathless.

Rob casually dialed Hugh and put the conversation on speaker.

"That's right. They were tall and black, and I could tell they were up to no good. You were always quiet. Never unkind, but quiet, so I knew something very wrong was going on. I've always heard what goes on in the dark comes out in the light, so I went to the electrical room for this complex right over there and cut the power for this whole courtyard so they couldn't see."

Loren put her hand on the woman's shoulder, but Nera hugged her tightly. "Ms. Nera, you're quite a lady."

"Oh, I'm more than that. Before I retired I was an electrical engineer for the power company, and I did the electrical work on this whole block back in '05, Ms. Loren. How's that for a black history moment?"

Both Rob and Loren broke into spontaneous laughter.

Nera's shoulders shook with pride. "Well, they got madder than a kicked hill of red ants. The electricity was already off to the building, and now they couldn't even use the parking lot lights. They were practically running from the building with furniture. I didn't know what else to do so I called the cops."

Loren's lack of confidence in the police showed in the expression on her face.

"Would you walk me home?" Nera asked them.

Rob nodded, and they strolled along with the slightly stooped black woman.

"The intruders got on the good foot and left, so right before dawn me and my friends, the old biddies we call ourselves, we got together and gathered some of your things for you."

Loren walked into Nera's first-floor apartment and saw her life, slightly burned around the edges, being tended to by a bunch of old ladies.

"Biddies, this is Loren and her boyfriend, what's yo' name?"

Rob couldn't stop the grin from spreading across his face. "Rob Hood."

"That's her boyfriend, Robin Hood."

By silent agreement, he and Loren decided not to correct Nera.

A woman stood and put her hands on her back and stretched. Her grin was welcoming.

"Well, come on in. Robin, Loren. I'm Lettie. I'm on picture detail. I own a photography studio, so I restored these for you the best I could. Have to say they came out real good."

Tears fell from Loren's eyes as she saw the pictures of her mother and father. She thought she'd lost them forever. She swept Lettie into a big hug and wept with joy. "Thank you for giving them back to me. I'm so very happy—I—I never thought I'd see them again."

Lettie patted her back as the emotion poured out of her. "Darling, I know. It's okay. It's all right now," the old woman said. Loren finally composed herself, and let Lettie go, taking another look at the pictures.

Rob put his arm around her and wiped her tears, kissing her temple.

"Robin, there've been hoodlum types lurking around today," Nera told him.

"Can you describe them?"

"Well, some men I can't understand. If Tullie wasn't so hard of hearing we would know. She knows seven languages. But it doesn't do us a bit of good if you can't hear, right, Tullie?" Nera said loudly.

Tullie was a small white woman who was sitting in an oversize rocker, pillows stuffed around her sides, knitting needles in her hands, asleep. Her eyes opened. "They were speaking a Nigerian language, common in Nigeria and Lagos. Is my tea ready yet?" she said in a language no one understood but Loren.

"How do you know, Tullie?"

Tullie answered and gestured with her bent fingers, nodding and pointing toward the window.

Everyone stopped moving and looked at Loren, who'd gone to Tullie's side. "What did she say?" Nera asked.

"She spoke to me in my native language, Lakota. I've never met a white woman who spoke Lakota," she said softly. "Tullie said she was a missionary in Lagos for ten years. She said they argued about whether to reburn my place, but that it would be declared arson and to just leave with what they had. She said her hearing is terrible but her eyes are keen as an eagle's. She got a license plate off a car and a truck."

Tullie had already drifted back to sleep.

"She's an interesting woman. I guess we should start believing her stories." Lettie smoothed Tullie's dress over her knees.

Loren bent down by Tullie and spoke to her in Lakota. Tullie's eyes fluttered open. They conversed quietly and Loren wrote something on her paper and Tullie drifted off to sleep again.

Loren gave Rob more information about the men and the vehicles and put the rest of the information in her purse.

"How do you afford to live here, if you don't mind my asking?" Rob said to Nera, putting his arm around Loren's waist when she returned to his side.

"I lived here with my husband until he died ten years ago. He was an architect. I own this place and have for years. They aren't going to get me out, not even with all their new rules and regulations about how many you can have in a home. I'm grandfathered in. Hell, I *am* the grandfather," Nera said, crinkling up her nose and laughing.

Loren rubbed Nera's back. "What a dear you are."

Two women emerged from the back and shuffled up front on canes. "There's some new men in the parking lot. The moving truck is still here. Well, this is *the* Loren Smith. How you doin'? I'm Myrtle, Myrt for short. This is Hester."

"I'm honored to meet you. Thank you all for saving my memories. Tullie said you found my safe?"

Myrtle nodded. "We had a devil of a hard time getting it out of your closet. I had to bring it back in my grandson's plastic wagon. It's all covered up and protected. It's on the deck."

Rob shook his head. "You ladies are amazing. Loren, is there anything you need in there right now?"

She shook her head. "I don't want to go out there and arouse suspicion."

Rob took her hand. "I'll send Ben for it tomorrow."

Nera shook her head sadly. "We couldn't handle the other furniture. But we got all your pictures and some of your clothes and your toiletries. They weren't taking your lotions. Those are expensive!"

Loren went over and embraced the woman, then hugged all the others. "I don't know how to thank you."

"Well," Nera said, "we go to the nursing home on Lenox Road on Thursdays for a dance. Maybe one Thursday you could come by and show us how to do our makeup. We might think that's a lot of fun."

"I want to walk like a model. I had my hip replaced so I can lift it now," Myrtle said, bent over a walker that had been in the corner.

"I would love to," Loren said.

Rob swallowed his laughter and they all looked at him. "Brilliant idea. Next Thursday I'll send a car for you ladies. How's a limousine sound?"

"Oh, mercy, a limousine." Myrtle stood straight. "I'm gonna finally ride in a limousine before I die. I'm gonna get my hair done, too."

Rob shook his head. "Ladies, I'm going to need you to watch Loren's stuff for another day. We're going to walk out of here, and Loren's going to pretend she's very sad. I'll have someone come back for her things. He's going to look like me because he's my twin brother, Ben, or my other brother, Zachary."

Loren opened her purse and pulled out a thousand dollars. "Nera, this is for you and the girls. Get your hair done and whatever else you want to do. But mostly it's in thanks for restoring these photos of my mom and dad. I'm eternally grateful."

"A thousand dollars. Plus the other hundred." Nera's mouth hung open. "Loren, you don't have to do this. I saw how upset you were. I was just trying to be nice, and that night all I could spare was ten dollars. You don't have to do this." Nera pushed the money along the countertop back at Loren.

"Oh, Nera, please? You gave me something when I had nothing. I am so touched by your generosity. It would mean so much to me if you'd take this money. Please? Do the other ladies need anything? Where do you all live?"

"We live here," Lettie said. "We don't have enough money to live alone so we share. We need that money, Nera. She's being real nice."

Loren took Rob's hand and he kissed her red nose. "I'm going to leave the money and you girls can talk it over and decide how to spend it." Loren took the two pictures she wanted the most and welled up. "I'm just so thankful to have these again. No money can replace them. Really. Thank you, Lettie, Myrtle, Hester and Tullie, when she wakes up, and you especially, Nera. I just really appreciate it."

"You're welcome," the ladies said in unison.

"Okay, Loren." Nera came and patted her on the back. "Don't cry no more. Robin..." She looked to Rob. "What you gonna do to the people who stole her stuff?"

"You know how the Robin Hood tale goes?"

"Yeah," Nera said. "You take from the rich and give to the poor. Well, could you remember us po' folks? Tullie really does need a hearing aid."

He nodded, noting the needs of five women in a three-bedroom apartment. "I won't forget."

They slipped out after long goodbye hugs, and Loren secured the pictures beneath her coat. She wiped her eyes and put her glasses back on. Rob exited the breezeway and saw Odesi, and tightened his grip on Loren's hand.

Loren noticed the change and spotted him. She lost her footing and slid down the steps, trying to break free of Rob's grasp.

Arrogantly, Odesi stood with his feet wide, a medallion on his chest, his hands on his waist, posing. "Loren, I want to speak to you!" Odesi yelled, as if he owned the land he was standing on.

Their hands separated and Loren turned to run in the opposite direction, when Rob caught her by her leg. "Loren, stop. Stop!"

"No, he's going to kill me!"

Chapter 21

"**I**'m not armed." Odesi walked confidently down the hill he'd been standing on. "I've come to reclaim what's mine. Loren, you brought this onto yourself. Now that we've been reunited, I will forgive you. But you must atone for your sins and ask for forgiveness."

They'd gotten to the car and Rob shoved Loren inside. "She doesn't want anything to do with you. This is your only warning. Stay away from her."

Odesi was nearly identical to Rob in height, but soft in muscular structure. He was model perfect, but that was only good for pictures. He was probably worthless where it counted in a real woman's life. Rob couldn't imagine him holding a woman's head through the first trimester of pregnancy as he had before DeLinda was killed. That job was probably too messy for this pretty boy.

"Most women want men who don't try to hurt them. No means no, bruh. So for the last time, leave Loren alone."

"You don't know my power, little man. I can do anything I want. You won't even have time to say goodbye."

Odesi lifted his hand and then looked around curiously. He signaled again, and when nothing happened, he began to back up, fear trumping confidence.

Rob stared him dead in the eye. "I gave a kill order, too. Your men are gone. You want to fight fair?" Rob tossed him a gun and threw his hands up just as the police surrounded them.

"You coward." Odesi laughed, his eyes reflecting pure hate. He dropped the gun as six guns were pointed at him.

"Am I?" Rob replied. "I'm not going to jail."

"I am Odesi Tunaotu," he said to the police, who shoved his face into the dirt. "I have diplomatic immunity." The Atlanta police didn't seem impressed. They took a statement from Rob and took Odesi away.

Rob got in the car and drove away and Loren said nothing. He stopped at the bank and she waited for him to open the door, stepping out only after he gave the all clear. Walking inside, she went straight to the vice president's office and straightened out her identity issue.

She withdrew a large sum of money, then walked out and got back into the car without a word to him. Loren worried her lip with her teeth until she bled, but she never said a word through the deliveries at the restaurants and fire station.

Finally they were alone and heading home. "What are you angry about?"

"I knew he would come and you antagonized him!" she exploded. "He's going to come after me and he's going to finish what he started. I'll be dead or you'll be dead and your family will blame me. I'm leaving tonight. It's not safe anymore. While he's locked up, I'm getting out of here."

"So that's what the big withdrawal was for. No, you're not leaving. You're not running anymore."

"Yes, I am, and you can't stop me." She folded her arms, then shielded her eyes as if the world was too much. Rob had seen scared women, but this was too much.

"You're giving him permission to chase you. The Hood team can stop him. We will stop him."

"You can't, Rob. You don't know his power. He'd given the order to kill you. What if one of his men had stayed behind and followed through?"

"Loren, those men were neutralized before the truck left. I stopped being a cop because they had too many rules. Hoods don't have the same rules and we do things our way. Odesi thought he was going to harm me not knowing who I am or what I do, but he would have died and he realized that. He doesn't know me and he doesn't know our strength. The best thing you can do is to let us help you."

"Rob, there's nobody left. If he takes you from your brothers and sisters, or Ben from Zoe and the rest of your family, I'll be filled with guilt for the rest of my life. It's only me left in my whole family."

She was trying to save him and he couldn't imagine anything more wonderful and equally sad, because she was doing it at the expense of her own happiness. "So you're not worth anything? Did he convince you of that? Why aren't you worth saving? Why aren't you worth having around?"

"Rob, it's just me. I can relocate and he won't find me. He couldn't find me for two years. I can start over. I can do anything, I realize that now. I've reinvented myself and I know how to do it, Rob. I just don't want anyone to be hurt because of me."

"You have to know you mean the world to Zoe. You're worth a whole lot. You don't have to run anymore, Loren."

"What happens when he shows up? What happens when just for the hell of it he kills someone because they know me? He gave an order for you to get killed! He's vindictive and I have to be smarter than him." She was so terrified her body was shaking.

"Loren, it's too late to run. Odesi declared war, and the Hoods aren't going to sit by and let his attempt on my life slide."

Her hands sought him. "Rob, you could come with me. I have enough money so that we can be comfortable—"

"No, baby. Hoods don't run. Now, Odesi may think he can scare you, and we're going to let him think that, but we're going to get him and when we do, he and his false claim of diplomatic immunity is going to cause him a world of trouble.

"What do you want, Loren?"

"What do you mean?"

"Out of all of this, what do you want to see happen? Running isn't an option."

The sadness that drifted off of her was tremendous. "Freedom. I want my freedom, Rob. Do you feel better now?"

He grabbed her arm. "Do you?"

"No, because I don't believe it's possible. Everything I've loved dies."

"Then you need to love bigger and you need to love more. We're going to the store. You have cakes to make."

"You can't possibly expect me to keep my regular routine after this."

"Yes, I do. Odesi isn't going to rob you of another moment of your life, baby. His reign of terror is over."

Rob pulled into the parking lot of a wholesale shopping center and parked his car, putting up the sun guard though clouds had overpowered the sun. He pressed the automatic seat button, moved his seat back and unbuckled his belt. Unbuckling hers, Loren reached for her door handle and yelped when Rob had her backward in his lap, his lips against her cheek. "Say it, Lakota Sky. You're not hiding anymore."

"I can—"

He kissed her with an urgency that came from inside his body. He would not lose her. He needed her to understand that. "You have to know he will come after you no matter if I'm there to protect you or not. Lakota, once you let go of your fear, he has no power. We're going in that store and we're going shopping and when we get home, we're celebrating my birthday. After that, I'm making love to you."

She stilled. "You are?"

He looked into her eyes. "Yes. Now say it," he whispered. "Say you trust me."

"I trust you." Tears ran into her hair. "Get him and put him in jail for good. I want my freedom back."

He touched his forehead to hers. "Come on. We've got a lot of work to do."

Rob exited the car and didn't see the presence of danger, but sensed it as Loren had earlier that morning. He took her hand and one crutch. He was getting rid of the thing today.

Chapter 22

Loren disabled the alarm to the house and she and Rob walked inside. "Today in that store I felt like everything was going to come down on my head."

"A couple times you did look a little green. You should have said something."

"Being out is still new for me. It's going to take time."

"Compared to last month or last year, how do you feel?"

"Better. I won't lie, but will I ever be one hundred percent? I don't know."

"You're doing well, Lakota. You have to remain positive."

She walked by him and tapped his thigh. "Okay, Mr. Positive. By the way, I'm moving you downstairs. No arguments. That was one of your original rules."

They headed back to the kitchen and started putting the food away.

"No, you're not."

"Yes, I am. We're not having a repeat of this morning."

"Then stop watering the plants."

"The plants love me. Zoe asked me to water them. I didn't mean for you to slip. How's your knee?"

"Fine."

"And your wrist?"

"Loren?"

Her hand was halfway out the bag. "Yes?"

"My everything is fine."

"If that's the case, then you don't need birthday food, cupcakes and birthday presents."

Rob shook his head. "Now you got jokes. You promised and I know you're not going back on your word. I've got to call the detectives in Ohio. Do you need me for anything?"

"No. I can take care of this. You want to walk outside for a while?"

He nodded and grabbed the crutch. "That's a good idea."

"Give me an hour to get this going and I'll join you."

Loren mixed the cake first, knowing what she had in mind would take a while to prepare. He only wanted one cupcake, but he'd done so much for her, one cupcake could be made from a box. And she would never do that. She added ingredients from memory, from the recipe her mother had taught her, making the glaze for the cake in a separate glass bowl. She didn't want the glaze to take on the flavor of the dish.

Dinner wouldn't take nearly as much time to prepare. She was serving tilapia. She hoped he liked the white fish. She'd bought jumbo shrimp and was making a sauce from scratch, too. Hopefully all of this was food he'd enjoy. While the cake was baking, she went upstairs and cleaned the floor, making sure the planter wasn't leaking anymore. Then she began the painstaking task of moving his clothes and toiletries to the lower bedroom where she'd been sleeping.

Rob might fuss, but he would lose this fight.

As she hung his clothes in the closet, a packet of pictures fell from the pocket of his jacket and she picked them up. She looked at the photographs and her breath caught as she saw DeLinda. Their similarities were startling. Their education was nearly alike and they'd both fallen in love with the same man.

Loren looked at the doorway as the pictures slipped to the floor.

How could she love Rob? He didn't know half of her life. She wasn't out of trouble. They'd been together barely three weeks. He didn't *know* her. He didn't know how her breath smelled in the morning after she forgot to brush. He didn't know how psycho she got around her period. He hadn't seen her naked. He didn't know that twice a year, the days of her mother's and father's deaths, she stayed in bed and cried a box of tissues away. Rob had no idea what her loving him could do to his life.

She folded her arms across her chest and tried to will her tears away. She didn't have to tell him. Once he caught Odesi, she could just vanish. Her father had left her the villa in Italy, and she had all of her mother's and father's money, plus her own. She would help the biddies from the apartment complex, and then she'd do what she'd come to know best. She'd disappear. That was the right thing to do. Unbidden tears fell and she wept for a few minutes before drying her face on her arms. Life sucked.

Her cell phone rang in the kitchen and she hurried to catch it. "Hello?"

"Ms. Smith, this is claims adjuster Brent Jenkins of Gillette Insurance Company, and we're prepared to settle the claim on your apartment."

"What's your offer, Mr. Jenkins?" She walked back to the bedroom and sat on the bed.

"One million dollars."

A million little shocks assaulted her skin. *A million dollars.* "Mr. Jenkins, my property was declared a total loss, isn't that correct?"

"Yes, that's correct, and you decided not to stay at the Red Hen Hotel. So that didn't decrease your insurance benefit."

She shook her head, sure the other fire victims didn't know that.

"Mr. Jenkins, isn't the building going to have to be demolished?"

"Yes, but there are units available in your complex. You can wait for yours to be rebuilt or you can buy into another unit. They've gone up, but you'll have to take that up with a Realtor."

"What about my rider?"

"What rider would that be? I'm not aware of any rider. Was it on jewelry or firearms?"

"No, Mr. Jenkins, I purchased a rider last month where I bought coverage that allows me to opt out of the home if it suffers catastrophic damage, which it has. I have a copy of that in my safety-deposit box. Regardless, I have two million dollars in coverage, Mr. Jenkins."

"Uh. I wasn't aware of any rider, Ms. Smith, and I'm only authorized to offer you the one million dollars."

"Who's your boss, Mr. Jenkins? I'd like to deal with him or her from now on."

"Her name is Jordan Burke. There's clearly been a mistake. I need to do some further investigation. I apologize, Ms. Smith. I'll have her give you a call."

"Before she calls, speak to my insurance agent, Toni Dempsey. Have your boss get all of my paperwork and know all the correct information. I don't mean to sound rude, but I have to make living arrangements, and I don't want to circle the trees with you all because you're unprepared. Have a nice day."

Loren ended the call and stood to find Rob in the doorway. "How long have you been there?"

"A minute. Why were you crying?"

"Because girls cry. You have sisters."

"You've met my sisters, they don't cry. They'd rather shoot people."

"I wish I was one of them."

"You're in a bad mood after talking to the insurance company? What happened?"

"They offered a million dollars, but I have a rider that bumps it to two if there's catastrophic loss, and a fire falls under that definition. At the suggestion of my agent, I took out the extra coverage when I installed the new ovens last month. I had to have the place inspected and new permits issued to do commercial cooking. The insurance company wants me to move into another apartment in my complex, but they're more expensive, and now that everyone knows I live there, I won't have any privacy. And my furniture has been stolen. I can't just replace all my stuff because a million dollars is all they're offering. That's garbage."

"A million," he said.

She nodded, wanting to leave the room, but he was standing in the way. "It sounds petty, but the point of buying such expensive coverage was if there was a catastrophe, I could replace everything. I bought that furniture as I traveled around the world. It didn't come from an assembly line."

He chuckled. "I hear you. Go on."

"Why do you think Odesi took my things?"

"To make you to come to him. He figures if he has it, he has leverage. He'll contact you to get it back. That's why he's writing a tell-all book on your life and why he bugged your car."

"What!"

"Last night when we stopped at the gas station, I heard the announcement on the radio about the book."

"Can he do that?"

"Yes, if it's unauthorized. He inked a six-figure tell-all book deal, but you can fight him in court. Others have won."

"Rob, he's trying to ruin me," she said grimly.

"He's trying to discredit you, but ultimately he wants you for himself. If you went to him and said, 'Odesi, I'm coming back, forgive me,' he'd stop long enough to tell the world he was right, then he might harm you and tell the story. He wants total control, then profit, and that's even worse. After I discovered your car was being followed, I discovered it was bugged. You'd gone into the store and I had Hugh scan it. We found the bug and disabled it, then went to the movies. Seeing Odesi's lieutenant was a coincidence."

"I don't believe in coincidences." Loren swept her hand through her hair.

"We escaped him, got home, and now we have to get Odesi where we want him. Odesi's still in jail, by the way."

Surprised, Loren gazed at him. "You're kidding. He's never spent the night in jail before. Not that I know of. He's going to be pissed off, Rob."

"I'm not scared of him. Still, there's no saying how long they're going to be able to keep him there. But he knows by now that the Hoods put him there. We have no choice but to finish this job. I called a meeting for tomorrow. Loren, we intend to end this."

"Is there nothing I can do to convince you otherwise?"

He shook his head. "I'm not afraid of him, and you'll stop being afraid once he's gone. What's going to happen with your apartment?"

"Mr. Jenkins is going to have his boss call me back. I want the money so I can find a nice, private place to live. Not some place where paparazzi can just walk in and people can bother me. That doesn't sound right. I think I want a house in a private subdivision or something like that."

She didn't want to say near him, but that's what she wanted.

The timers went off on the stove, and she started for the door when Rob saw the photos of DeLinda.

"Rob, I moved your things down here and these fell out of your pocket. I'm sorry to have looked at your personal property. We just look so much alike. It's surreal."

"Does that bother you?"

She got to the door. "How could it not? I'm looking at my face and it looks like I'm dead."

Loren moved past him and went into the kitchen. The cupcakes were a warm golden brown and she put the trays on top of cooling racks.

"DeLinda isn't you. You're not her."

"Have you ever considered that the person who killed her didn't know that?"

Before the words were out of her mouth, her gaze flew back to his and she ran to the room and snapped up the pictures.

"Rob, do you think so?" The possibility was there and Loren held her chest. "What if a hit man got confused? When did she die?"

"No, Loren. Don't take this on, too. Hit men kill, they don't rape. The detectives in Ohio have a person of interest. He's never said a word about you. He lost his land to the Native Americans because artifacts were found on it. They believe he's been harboring this hate for years and finally acted upon it."

Her shoulders finally settled down. "That's terrible. Didn't he get compensation?"

Rob looked at the photos, too. "He was compensated, but he feels as if he should have gotten more considering what was found on the land."

Loren stared at DeLinda and caressed her cheek. "She was an innocent bystander who had no idea why she was being raped and killed. How awful."

Loren prayed for his wife in Lakota, and Rob felt tears rush to his eyes. If there was a better woman on earth, he wouldn't find her. She finally gave him the picture.

"You can't take responsibility for everything that happens to everyone." He caressed her hair, something she'd come to accept as a sign of comfort. She caught her breath and straightened his shirt, which she'd bunched in her fists.

"I don't want to cause you any pain."

"I feel the same about you," he said.

She wrapped her arms around his waist. "I need to call Zoe. I've got to find someplace to live."

"You need to get some sleep. You were up early cleaning and then we were out. Now you're worrying about where to live. Slow down. Everything is going to be all right."

"I've got to put dinner on. We still need to get a walk in. Doctor's orders."

She looked up into his face and wondered how she could fall in love so quickly.

"Yes, I'll walk. Then we deliver the cakes to Phillipe. After that we celebrate. You haven't forgotten, have you?"

"One dinner, dance, cupcake and movie, Mr. Hood."

Rob loosened from her, and she missed the connection she'd finally made with the man who'd finally given her peace and promised freedom. He stepped back on his good foot and pulled her up and into his arms. "There'll be more."

"Yeah?" she whispered.

"Definitely."

Chapter 23

Loren sampled the tilapia and cast a quick glance at the grilled asparagus. The cream of avocado soup was perfect, and the fresh lime margaritas were ready to pour. The Caesar salad was crisp with freshly ground Parmesan cheese, and she'd grilled tender filet mignons just in case Rob wanted surf and turf. Loren lit the candles on the table, then rushed up the stairs to find her shoes.

Grabbing the red heels from the other night's dance-off between the girls, she bolted back down the stairs and entered the lower-level powder room to put the final touches on her makeup. She couldn't remember when it mattered more for her to look and feel good for a man.

She got close to the mirror and lined her eyes, loving the way the deep purple dress with the sunken vee accentuated her body. The scars weren't visible, but enough of her was showing to titillate. Tonight she wanted to be provocative. *You're gorgeous. I love your smile. The scars don't matter to me.*

You're ugly. Nobody will ever want you again.

Rob's and Odesi's words from when he'd seen her at her father's grave site a year ago battled in her head, and she cut off the bathroom light and let them fight it out. The brutal slugfest reached a feverish pitch and she held her temples with the heels of her hands, wishing she could figure out which one to believe. She inhaled deeply and put the lights back on and looked at her face. She'd extended the liner too far. She dipped a Q-tip in water and erased the mistake, then went over it with foundation.

He knocked on the door. "Ms. Smith, are you ready for dinner?"

She glanced at her purple dress and red shoes. Nothing was perfect, but Rob hadn't ever asked her to be perfect.

She opened the door. "Yes, Mr. Hood, I'm ready."

Rob drank in the sight of her and Loren couldn't recall ever being so admired. "You look beautiful."

She turned around slowly. Not like a model. Like any woman would for the man who liked her.

"Oh, baby," he said, a smile in his voice. "That's even better."

Long ago Loren remembered being impulsive, but life had worn that out of her. Now she easily took his hand and moved into his arms. "You make me feel like a desirable woman."

"That's because you are."

His words worked their way into her lungs, and she held them there before exhaling. Still, she kept what was necessary to live.

"Are you hungry?" she asked.

"I am. Whatever you fixed smells good."

Impulsively she clapped. "Go ahead and sit down. I'll serve you."

The table for eight was set with them at opposite ends of the table, and Loren had used fresh fruit in bowls for the centerpiece. She brought the food into the dining room and saw that he'd reset the table with them sitting side by side.

"I thought we'd be more comfortable."

"It's your birthday." She admired the way he was dressed in khaki pants and white shirt, and wearing Usher's latest cologne for men, an aphrodisiac if she ever smelled one.

She felt shy, serving him in the skimpy dress and four-inch

heels. But his visual admiration pummeled Odesi's audacity. She put him out of her mind and focused on her new love. The joy it brought her and the man who brought it to her.

Rob blessed the food and they ate.

"Are you enjoying your dinner?" she asked, barely able to stay in her chair.

He shook his head. "No, I'm loving it. Everything is delicious."

Loren blushed from her feet to the roots of her hair. "You're just saying that. Who can't cook steak?"

He looked at her. "This is the best birthday I've had in a long time. And you are simply gorgeous." His words were the final knockout blow to Odesi's evil hold. The torture was over.

Loren leaned over and kissed Rob's cheek. "Thank you."

"For what?"

"Everything. You know, you keep telling me I'm gorgeous, but you're pretty hot yourself." She put her fork down. "You're extraordinarily handsome."

He pulled her chin to him and kissed her lips. Rob's touch was tender and sent thrills down her neck to her back. She could get used to this kind of desire that she felt for him. It seemed to increase by the moment.

She caressed his cheek. "Eat. I want you to enjoy your dessert."

"You are dessert."

Loren moaned, and finished her dinner with her hand resting comfortably on his knee.

Dessert was served in crystal goblets filled with cake and ice cream, and Rob blew out his sparkling candle before digging in. "Baby, this is delicious." His eyes were so gentle she got lost in the glow.

"Thank you."

"No, I really mean it. You should sell this cake. You'd make a killing."

"It's personal. Everything you do in life doesn't have to be for money. That recipe is my mother's and I only make it on special occasions. If I ever have a daughter, I'll pass it down to her and she'll make it for her children."

Admiration filled his eyes. "I never thought of it that way. I'm glad you consider me special enough to have made it for me."

"Of course." Loren waited until he was finished before she pushed her chair back and extended her hand to Rob. "It's time we dance."

"We?" He laughed. "You're supposed to be dancing for me. Remember, I'm injured."

She scoffed. "I don't think so. You've been a bad boy all week. So you just stand here and take your dance like a man." She took a big sip of her margarita and hit the remote, one of her favorite songs, "I Like the Way You Move," by Earth Wind & Fire and Kenny G, starting.

Loren moved seductively around him and mouthed the words, never breaking eye contact. She brushed her body against his chest in slow motion and kissed under his chin, then put his hands on her hips as she moved seductively against him. Kissing him deeply, she broke away to run her hands down his body and then back up.

Holding on to his waist, she did a seductive grind, then came around, her hands on his neck, her back to his front, doing a twisting curl to the floor until the music faded. Then she stood and kissed him. "Rob, take me to bed."

"Oh, baby, if I could only carry you…"

"We'll do the next best thing," Loren suggested. The crutch forgotten, they walked with his arm around her waist and made it to the threshold of the bedroom. Loren put her hands on his shirt and guided him inside.

"You are a vision of exceptional beauty."

Loren walked with him over to the bed and Rob sat down. She stayed within the confines of his arms, comfortable there.

He guided the purple shift from her shoulders and she tried to calm her nerves.

"There's nothing to be nervous about," he assured her, planting kisses between her breasts. Their lips met in a rapturous kiss that sent hints of ecstasy down her legs. Not only did Rob's lips possess hers, he knew what to do with his hands, too. She perched on his good leg, their lips locked tight, his tongue connecting with hers in the promise of greater passion. Loren gave in to that feeling, letting the thin straps of her dress slide completely off her arms. She wanted Rob so much, she heard her ragged breath and, embarrassed, buried her face in his neck, but he wouldn't have it. He turned and sought her lips, adjusting her in his lap until he was cradling her and could have as much of her mouth as he wanted.

He paused for a second and was quiet. Rob stroked her hair, then down her nose, then along her jawbone. Then, with his finger, he bumped up her chin and their lips connected again. His eyes said all the words he hadn't voiced. To him she was lovely, beautiful, gorgeous.

Loren snaked her arm around his neck, desiring him more than anyone she'd ever known. She was at his mercy as he plundered her mouth, then kissed her face and hair. Rob was making her feel again in places where scars had left her numb.

His lips strayed to her shoulder, and she let herself relax into the pleasure of his wet kisses. His hands cupped her breasts, and she moved away and stood up, giving him the best angle so he could bury his face between her breasts. She could feel him laughing, and she kissed his face and looked down at him. "What are you doing in there?" she asked.

"This feels good."

Loren stepped back and closed her eyes and pulled the dress over her torso and let it fall to her feet. She kicked it away and stood before him, naked. Nobody except doctors had seen her unclothed.

"Keep your eyes closed," he told her.

Loren felt her esteem start a free fall from the height of the Eiffel Tower. That's where Rob's words had lifted her.

She felt him get up and could sense him moving around the room, and she wondered if she could make a dash to the bathroom and preserve what was left of her ego.

Then she felt him undressing, his shirt breezing past her to the floor. His socks and pants landing in the vicinity of her dress. His boxers hitting the floor in a whisper by her feet.

"Come here," he said.

Loren finally opened her eyes and saw the freestanding antique mirror Zoe kept in the room. He'd maneuvered it close to the bed. She looked at Rob suspiciously. He'd pulled every cover off the bed except the sheets and he was completely naked. Even the knee brace was gone.

"What are you doing?" she demanded.

Her hands were across her middle and he tugged at her arms. "There's nothing to be afraid of, baby."

She kicked off her heels and crawled into the center of the mattress. The evidence of his desire grazed her thigh, and she welcomed it with warm hands. His smile was so damned glorious. They both looked in the mirror, and Rob came up behind her on his left knee. "That's you. You're beautiful. Say it. Say 'I'm beautiful.'"

"Rob," she admonished, taking his hand as he traced her scars with his finger.

His hands caressed her cheeks and shoulders and stopped at her breasts, where he cupped them, and his thumbs slowly moved to her nipples. She leaned back into him, loving the way they looked together.

"I mean it. You have to believe you're beautiful. These scars don't define who you are. Whether you're scarred inside or out, you're still a beautiful person."

She'd turned partially away and he turned her back toward the mirror and touched each scar. "Look at them. They're a part of your body, but there's nothing wrong with you. Lakota, look at them. Say it, 'I'm beautiful.'"

"I'm beautiful." The words didn't even sound true coming from her. Distracted by the bathroom light, Loren wanted to take refuge in the room behind the closed door. She wanted to run because it was a lie.

The scars were ugly and red, imbedded into her cream-colored skin, but what he was doing felt good and right. So she watched his hands and his face. She focused on his features because she'd be able to tell if he were lying by his expression.

Rob traced the thickest scar, the one that wound like a rope and had the most scar tissue. It itched and ached and reminded her of that fateful night so often. When it hurt, she thought of her mother. When it ached she thought of Odesi. She hated this scar more than any of the others and she wanted to turn away, but Rob's gaze held her captive. Her stomach retracted.

"Say it," he demanded.

"I'm beautiful." Tears welled in her eyes and her head dropped. "I don't believe it. I can't lie to you."

"You're beautiful, Lakota Sky, do you hear me? Beautiful! Don't give him any more power over you. Who's your mother?"

"Wenona Sky Thunderhawk."

"Was she beautiful?"

Loren nodded.

"Look at yourself. And your father?"

"Arnold Smith."

"Was he beautiful?"

She nodded, swallowing more tears than she shed. Her spirit grew lighter the more he talked.

"Are you the offspring of Wenona Sky Thunderhawk and Arnold Smith?"

"Yes, I am."

"Two beautiful people cannot make an ugly baby. It's impossible. I think Wenona and Arnold would agree with me. Lakota Sky Thunderhawk Smith. Are you beautiful?"

Lakota looked at her face and her body, her hair and her hands. She crawled to the edge of the bed and stared at herself. Her wet eyes, red nose, her splotchy cheeks and her creamy skin. Six scars marked her torso, but that didn't stop her from being her mother and father's daughter. She was still Lakota Sky Thunderhawk Smith.

She looked at Rob in the mirror. "I'm beautiful."

"Damn right you are."

She crawled back to him and he traced the smallest scar, the most sensitive of the injuries, and she giggled despite herself, taking him by surprise, and he pushed her down and licked it. She curled and he assaulted each one as she wiggled. "Look in the mirror and say it, Lakota."

She looked in the mirror and saw her own face, devoid of studio makeup, full of real passion and desire that wasn't photographer-manufactured. This was real. "I'm beautiful."

His tongue caressed her scars—the things she had thought were the ugliest parts of her. He loved on them as if they were nothing, until they became nothing. Then he joined with her, and he understood the tears she cried weren't for ugliness, but for the beauty he'd helped her see.

Rob watched Lakota sleep and knew he could never give her up. He'd fallen in love with her, and he wondered where she'd been since he'd become single. A year ago, a month ago, nobody would have been able to tell him he'd have been in love with a woman so opposite him, but he wanted her so badly he couldn't describe the depth of his desire.

She was afraid of her own shadow, yet he wanted to help her discover the treasures behind closed doors. Some would say she was seriously damaged goods, but wasn't he?

Rob caressed her back as she slept and Loren lifted her head. "What?"

He shook his head. "I didn't say anything."

"What are you thinking?" she asked, wiping her eyes as she sat up on her knees.

She was beautiful now more than ever before.

"That we should be asleep or doing something else besides talking."

She reached for him. "Well, let's make love like two uncivilized people."

"This is my dream come true." Rob rolled on top of her and she cupped his ass. "You're an ass woman. I knew I'd convert you."

He laughed as she swept her hands over his bottom again and again.

"Rob, stop teasing me."

"What?" he asked, lifting her leg, holding her knee under his arm. Loren shook with wanting.

"Take me."

"Gladly," he said, and pushed into her.

With her leg up, penetration was deeper, and she felt him in places she'd never felt anyone.

He pushed in again and she cried out in exquisite torture. Rob knew exactly what he was doing. Loren moved with him, accepting his thrusts, his lips setting her shoulders on fire. She couldn't help kissing him. Her tongue sought his in a coupling that seemed to spin out of control. They were moving and her head was soon off the bed, and she could see herself in the mirror, her hair cascading in wild curls over the side of the mattress.

Then he touched the swollen center of her desire and her climax spiraled and burst.

Loren grabbed Rob, and in Lakota, words of love fell from her lips as he came, too. Loren held him until she regained control of herself. "This is beautiful and so good," she told him, searching and finding the blankets and pulling them up to cover their bodies. "We're civilized people."

Rob pushed the covers away. "I want to look at you. Civilized be damned."

Loren couldn't believe it, but she wanted him again. "I totally agree."

Chapter 24

Loren lay in the bed, talking on the phone to Zoe while Rob got ready for his meeting. "Why can't I get up, Rob?"

"Because you're watching the show *How to Look Good Naked*."

"Zoe, did you hear that? It was on a cable channel, and I didn't have cable in my apartment."

"For a former fashion model, you are so behind the times." Zoe laughed in Loren's ear.

"I don't hear you," Loren told her best friend, laughing. The mirror that she'd come to avoid was now at the end of the bed, and she saw herself as she lounged in the comfort of a sea of pillows. She'd never been so comfortable naked. She snuggled beneath the comforter. "How's Ben?"

Zoe pretended to choke. "You're asking about Ben? He's fine. He left early to get your stuff from some old ladies and, boy, did he have stories. They love you! He did say one hit on him."

"That was probably Myrtle. She got a new hip. I promised to give them lessons on makeup and then they're going to a dance at the senior center. Myrtle wants to model."

"I go out of town and you're taking applications to replace me as your best friend."

"Never, Zoe. You'll always be my best friend."

"You sound like your old self again. I'm so glad you found a reason to smile. I swear, I tried so hard to get you out of your depression."

"I know, Zoe. But I was scared of Odesi."

"Why'd you date him, honey? He seems so unlike you."

Loren had asked herself that question a thousand times. "He represented everything that *was* different. He was bold and had that dark side and photographers loved the two of us together. We booked well as a couple. I had an agent to fight for me, but once they leave the set, about anything goes. With him there, nobody bothered me with nonsense."

"So he protected you?"

"He did, until his mentality changed."

"What happened?"

"Drugs, of course. He started using and making gross errors. I started getting jobs and making more money than he did. I was booked for major assignments, and he wasn't getting more than catalog calls. He became insulted and the worse he felt, the worse he treated me."

"What happened after your famous dance with D'Arby?"

"That was the icing on the jealousy cake. Odesi didn't come home for days. I'd heard he'd been fooling around, and I was furious. I went through his office and found pictures of girls and phone numbers and I started calling, looking for him. The truth about his sexcapades came to me from everywhere."

"Why didn't you call the police? Why didn't you leave?"

"I was in Monaco. I was in mourning for my mother. He walked in as if it were any ordinary day and demanded I be with him. I confronted him and he blew me off. We fought. You know the rest."

"He should be locked up."

"I know, but when the police let him get away, I thought it was best that I protect myself and go it alone. But Rob says he can get him. I'm just going to believe him."

"So you trust him?"

Zoe had to bring up the one thing she'd struggled with since she'd met Rob. "As much as I can."

"Is that enough, Loren? Because these Hood men require complete trust. Complete belief that they're going to help you get through whatever you're struggling with."

"I do, Zoe."

"You just be sure."

"What are you doing today?" Loren asked.

"I've come to learn that when they have meetings, don't make plans. I may see Ben and I may not see him until the next day. I'm going to work. Either way, he hooked a sista up before he left."

They both laughed and Rob walked out of the bathroom, using the cane. "You look good," Loren told him, unable and unwilling to keep the intimacy out of her voice.

"Don't try to entice me back into bed with you. I have a meeting."

"I know, but they won't be here for another hour."

"I have to get ready, woman!" he wiggled his eyebrows, looking for the right shoes.

"I am ready. I'm still naked, and I'm clean. See?" She lifted the cover to show him. "Plus, it's naked Friday all day today."

"Oh, goodness. I think I'm bleeding from the ear. I'm sure of it," Zoe said.

Loren had forgotten about her friend. "Sorry, Zoe. Rob, Zoe is bleeding from the ear after listening to us."

Rob took the phone. "I seriously doubt that after I walked in on you and Ben— Oh, I thought so."

Loren looked at him, her eyes wide, accepting the phone. "Tell me. What were they doing? She's such a prude. Do they have naked Friday's, too?"

"That's so sexy," Zoe said. "Ben's going to think you two are so cute when I give him a full report. Uh, when I can I come home?"

"Rob, Zoe wants to know when she can come home?"

"We'll let her know after the meeting."

"I heard him," Zoe replied.

"Good. Ooh... The show is on. Call me later, Zoe. Love you." Loren hung up the phone and pushed up on the pillows. "Rob?"

"Yes, baby?" Rob grabbed his notes and glanced at them, then looked in his briefcase.

She spoke Lakota to him until he sat down beside her on the bed and gave her his full attention. "Yes, dear? You have my full and undivided attention."

"I won't be angry if you don't catch him. And I want you to take this." She gave him an envelope. "I'm not showing off or trying to throw money around, or telling you how to do your job. But catching somebody like him is going to cost money, so I'd like to invest money into Hood Investigations to find Odesi and... disable him. You asked me to trust you and I trust you. You don't work for me.

"I'd like to be a silent investor with no authority to say how or what goes on in your company. If you don't find him, then the money is written off for me as a bad debt. You can talk it over with the other principles in the company. This silent, nonvoting partnership would only be for this case, and that's all." Her throat was dry and she really wanted to rub her eyes. Rob hadn't said a word. "What do you think?"

The beige envelope sat on the bed between them, and she wondered if she'd just made the second most-monumental mistake of her life. Rob pursed his lips and looked at the envelope. He picked it up and slid it through his fingers.

"Come here," he said, his eyes serious. "What do you want first? A kiss or a hug?"

Loren launched herself at him and he caught her and held her tight. "Oh, my goodness, you had me so scared. I thought you were going to get angry. Your face was so serious." She kissed his whole face. "You're welcome, love."

"I wish I had time," he breathed into her neck, his hands roaming her nude body. He stopped and just held her close. "They're going to be here any minute."

"We can go fast," she told him, yearning, needing him again. "Before they break in."

Rob laughed, her mouth too good to pass up. She needed to be free to love him.

Loren got his pants off enough and a condom on and Rob plunged into her. "Faster, Rob. I hear something. Your brothers are coming in."

"You come first," he breathed, his hands caressing her nipples and her lips, her head hitting something hard. She moved the remote, accidentally taking the TV off Mute.

She heard Odesi's voice from the TV and it disrupted their rhythm. "I just want my wife back, unstable as she is," he said. "Loren Smith is my wife."

The spirit of Odesi invaded their bedroom. Rob slid out of her and he looked confused, as if he didn't know her. She wanted to shove the TV out the window if it would decimate Odesi.

He was lying again, but his words were like a fast-moving venom. Rob didn't know whom to believe. Loren had never told him she was married to Odesi. He stood up, holding his head. "I didn't just hear that."

She reached for his wrists, but then drew her hands back and had the unreasonable desire to cover all of herself. "It isn't true. It was a ceremonial wedding off the island of Bora Bora. We were going to get married, but the ceremony was never legalized."

"That's crazy. Either you're married or you're not. I would never touch another man's wife."

Panic rose. This was Odesi's plan all along: to wreak havoc in whatever life she had and to destroy her. "Rob, please let me explain. The ceremony that was performed isn't legal in the U.S. You have to return to your home country and get married within thirty days of that ceremony, and we didn't do that. Odesi's doing this for publicity."

"Why would he do that? No one is that desperate."

"He is. Obviously he is."

Rob walked away from her, fixing his clothes, staring at her then at Odesi on TV. "Are you one hundred percent positive the wedding isn't legal?"

"Of course I'm sure. The law states you have to have been on the island for at least thirty days before the ceremony is performed and we weren't. Or return to your country and have the ceremony performed there. We did neither. He tried to kill me in Monaco before we ever made it back here."

Her hands shook and she held them as Rob walked into the bathroom and washed up. Their lovemaking seemed ridiculous now, so she straightened the bed and reached for the terry shift she'd used after her shower in the morning. It covered her from breast to thigh, but was better than nothing. She sat on the corner of the bed, waiting for him to either lose his temper, give her the cold shoulder or, worse, reject her altogether.

Loren held her breath and waited. One of those moods was going to walk out of the bathroom with Rob. Odesi only had two moods: hot and cold, and considering he'd been the only man she'd been with, she knew tantrums well. Loren grabbed the stray pillows off the floor and quickly tidied the room, then pulled out some clothes. Their little fantasy land might just be over.

"What are you doing?" he asked.

She took a deep breath and strove for a calm voice. "I thought…I thought things had changed. I know you're probably wondering why I didn't tell you. You told me about DeLinda, and it would have been the perfect time to tell you about…him. But I was ashamed that someone I put my faith in tried to kill me. I never wanted to admit that I could have loved someone who would maim and attempt to murder me. It's crazy, but that's why. I owe you an apology, and I'm sorry, but I thought after we got to know each other better we could talk about those things more. Otherwise, I'm just a woman you met briefly last year and then again three weeks ago who's got a lot of drama in her life. So that's why."

He closed his eyes and took her into his arms. "I wish you had told me. I do. Especially since he's making announcements to the world. But this won't change anything. We'll have time to talk later. As for today, let me focus on this meeting. We haven't been together for a month and a lot's gone on. So we have some catching up to do."

"Do you need me to explain anything to anyone?"

He looked serious. "No. You're watching TV." He took the clothes from her hands and hung them up, then held the covers while she got into bed. "Mute the TV anytime he comes on, and you're naked all day."

They both heard the alarm bells beep.

Loren stood on the bed and hugged Rob so hard she thought she'd break him.

"I think I'm the luckiest girl in the world."

"Yo, where's my future wife? Loren, do you remember me?"

"That's Zachary," Rob said, reluctantly pulling away from her, his fingers in her hair. "I'd better go. Watch TV and get used to being beautiful and naked. I'll be back."

Loren had not prayed much since that fateful night, and had

been surprised when Rob had blessed their dinner. But right then she felt compelled to fold her hands and thank God for Rob and the feeling of peace that embodied her.

When she was finished, she lay down and watched the show. She was amazed at the remarkable women who were brave enough to go on TV and tell their story to the world.

Anxiety built inside of her, and she sighed to rid her body of the weighty emotion. She pushed the blankets off herself and stood in front of the mirror. She stared at her body and the scars. Her eyes were squinted and her nose scrunched. She looked harder and straightened her face. This was her body and she needed to learn to be happier with it. The scars weren't all that made her.

Her phone rang and she grabbed it. "Hello?"

"Ms. Smith? It's Jordan Burke from the Gillette Insurance Company."

"Ms. Burke, I've been expecting your call."

"Yes, you spoke with my colleague recently and he unfortunately gave you some incorrect information. Your policy is for two million dollars. And that claim has been filed."

"That's very good news, Ms. Burke. How long will it take to pay on the claim?"

"About a week. If you need accommodations, we can recommend several extended-stay hotels. We can also make funds available for clothing and other necessities. We understand your home was a total loss and what wasn't lost in the fire was stolen."

"That's correct."

"Have you filed a police report?"

"No, I just found out about the theft yesterday. I'm still trying to get my credit cards working."

"Your home has been condemned and will be paid off. But

in the meantime, I can have a two thousand dollar check couriered to you, Ms. Smith."

She sounded sympathetic and apologetic. "Thank you, Ms. Burke, but I'm okay. I just need to know that my housing situation is being dealt with. A week from today, will I be getting the check?"

"Yes, ma'am. Things will be resolved. We've already received the necessary reports, and your claim will be paid within the week."

"Thank you. Please e-mail me a confirmation of our conversation, and I appreciate your call."

"You're welcome. Best to you, Ms. Smith."

"Thank you." Loren sat back, relieved that her housing situation was near conclusion. Now she'd just have to find another home, though she had no idea where she wanted to live. She thought about Rob's neighborhood and smiled, embarrassed. He might not want her living down the street from him. Maybe she'd go back to Italy like she'd done every year until the incident.

She picked up the pillow Rob had slept on and smelled it. She couldn't stand being away from him. How could she live in Italy?

She dialed her agent. "Hi, Dionne, it's Loren."

"Darling, it's been nearly three weeks. I was just calling you. Don't pick up your second line."

"How are you, Dionne?"

"How am I? You're the star of the hour! How are you?"

"I'm quite happy."

"I've never had one of my girls tell me she's happy. Not in forty years in this business. You should be happy, too. I got a call from a Chef Phillipe, and I knew things were changing. That dog of a man Odesi has been after me for years to tell him where you were and I never would. Never. Your phone number is the only one I've ever memorized. I never logged it into my phone in case it ever got stolen."

Loren appreciated her discretion. "What did the chef say?" she asked.

"Chef Phillipe said you agreed to bake for his restaurant. He's been wanting to do a line of cooking apparel, but didn't have the right vehicle. *You* are that vehicle. After speaking with him, I immediately got on the phone and talked to Duffy, and this morning she brought in some designs I think you're going to love."

"You're kidding?" Loren said, laughing. "Duffy wants to design cooking apparel for me? I'm so flattered."

"Yes," Dionne assured her. "This is a brilliant idea. She shot me some ideas and I e-mailed them over to you at that bizarre e-mail address you gave me last year when I sent your statements. Once you make some selections, I'll send them to Phillipe. And while you chew on that idea, I called my friends at my husband's network, and they want you to do a cooking show."

Loren fell backward on the bed, still holding Rob's pillow. "Dionne, you'd better not be lying to me."

"Darling Loren, after what you've been through, I wouldn't lie."

A million things ran around in Loren's head. "In Atlanta?" she asked softly.

"Yes, you won't have to go anywhere."

"Dionne, I'll do it."

Her agent gasped. "Did I hear the elusive Loren agree to something?"

Loren laughed and pushed her hair out of her face. "You did, Dionne. Because that suits me. I wanted to do something else besides modeling. I've been inspired by this fabulous show where the women learn to love their bodies and dress in more flattering ways."

"Loren, darling, what are you telling me?"

She looked at herself in the mirror. "Dionne, I'm ready to tell my story."

"Photos, too?" she asked softly.

Loren closed her eyes, but her heart was at rest. "Yes." She took a deep breath. "Dionne, my name is actually Lakota Sky Thunderhawk."

Loren thought she heard a small sob from her agent. "Very good, darling. Can I say I'm very proud of you?" Dionne was crying.

Loren nodded, welling up, too. "Yes. Dionne, Rob Hood is in the process of trying to catch Odesi, and he's vowed to take him down. They want to do this very soon, but I don't know when. Regardless of what happens with Odesi's capture, I would appreciate it if you were here with me."

"I'll be on the next flight to Atlanta. Meet me at my husband's network studio tomorrow. Loren, who's helping you get Odesi? Tell me his name again."

"My boyfriend, Rob Hood. He promised, and he's not ever broken his word to me."

Dionne cleared her throat. "Well, I love him already. I'll call when I get settled in my hotel."

"Thank you, Dionne. For everything."

"There's no need. I adore you, darling. Let's bury that bastard."

Chapter 25

"How much is the check for again?" Zach asked.

"A half million dollars."

They sat outside on the deck, basking in the crisp air and morning sun. Hugh sat opposite Rob and Ben, and they all stared at the envelope Loren had given Rob.

"She wants nonvoting partnership. Why doesn't she just hire us?" Ben asked.

"Because she doesn't want things to get weird between us. We didn't start out like you and Zoe, and so Loren thinks if she gives us a check for expenses and she's a nonvoting partner, then she's working with us and we're not working for her."

Hugh nodded. "She doesn't want you to think she's holding money over your head. She's got bank."

"She doesn't want any profit." Rob explained about the reward in Monaco.

"I say we take our usual fee and refund the rest," Hugh said. "We have to justify all expenses to the accountant and the government, and we can't split hairs. Ben, I've been on this "unofficially" while you were out of town. You might think Rob's too close to the situation, but he's telling you the truth. This guy is dangerous."

Hugh turned his computer around and began his presentation. "Odesi Tunaotu, thirty years old, was born in Ethiopia to an African father and a missionary mother who was later killed. His father later became an attaché and now is ambassador to the

UN. He enjoys diplomatic immunity and his only son exploits the privilege. He's been accused of rape, attempted murder, sodomy, harassment, pedophilia, trespassing, assault with intent to do bodily harm and vandalism."

"If she wasn't his only victim, why is he still walking around?" Zach asked, leaning back, his face serious when he was usually the family clown.

"Because these crimes have taken place over the course of his life, and in different countries. His father has done a good job of buying his son out of trouble," Hugh filled in.

"Has anyone pressed charges that have stuck?" Ben asked.

"Not really." Rob stood up and did twenty knee stretches. "That's why we have to develop a sophisticated plan that will be so bulletproof his father can't get him off. We need a confession."

Ben laughed. "Just from working Zoe's case we know how hard it is to get a confession, and we haven't had one since. What did you have in mind?"

"Odesi's hyped up about this book deal. What if we were to pretend to be his publisher and get his confession under the auspices of confirming the details of the story?" Hugh suggested.

The guys tossed the idea around. "That might work," Ben said. "But would he be dumb enough to do that? And who would he give it to? Not any of us, and the Hood Trap Team looks just like us."

Rob found himself smiling. "I've got the perfect women that helped us while Ben and Zach were away. Ice and a couple of her friends are in the TV business. I believe Loren's agent has a TV station down here, too. They can handle a ruse such as this."

"Do you think Loren would help?" Zachary asked.

Rob looked up and there was Lakota in the kitchen, clothed

in a robe, stirring cake batter. She'd piled her hair on top of her head. She waved to him and he waved back. "I don't want her traumatized any further. Odesi maimed her. When I say she's scared, I mean it. She wants to run and hide, so I don't want him anywhere near her." Rob stopped himself from rubbing his stomach.

"How many times did he stab her?" Zachary asked quietly.

"Six times. That's why she stopped modeling. She believes she's ugly, and she's taking baby steps in getting over that fear. Zoe was her only friend until me. She likes the Trap Team, and the new lady you guys will meet. Her name is Ice. When we saw Loren last year, she was, and still is to some extent, an agoraphobic. At that time she was only leaving her apartment twice a week."

"So he's paying in Hood cash. That's times ten," Zach confirmed.

Ben shook his head. "We're taking it all. Hugh told me he put a hit on Rob when he and Loren went to get her belongings from her apartment. He doesn't get to live *and* keep his assets. He gets to barely keep his life and nothing else. Or he gets to have nothing—no life...nothing."

Rob held up his hands. "As much as I want this man gone, we're playing this by the books. I'm also bringing the cops in on this one because of the international charges from the past. My hope is that he'll be charged in Monaco, and the charges will stick. Maybe women in other countries will see what we've done and come forward, too. Seriously, we don't need any problems."

Hugh agreed. "Ice will be a great help here. She's got Homeland Security clearance, and I've been working on helping her get her record clean from her last job. She was a great employee and Tunaotu did a job on her. I just e-mailed Odesi that his editor is coming to Atlanta and wants to meet him," Hugh said.

Ben jumped up. "We haven't even finished the plan."

"You don't know how badly I want this guy. He has a meeting in two days." Hugh rubbed his hands together. "Let's get this show on the road. He tried to throw Loren off a balcony, he bugged the car and he put a hit on Rob. If I hadn't been here, Rob would have walked out of Loren's apartment building into a straight ambush."

Rob put a calming hand out to Ben, who heeded the spirit of the gesture. "He's right. I'm ready to take him down."

Loren waved to Rob from the door and he walked over. She handed him a pan of food for the men as they talked. He passed the food to Ben, who carried it to the table. Rob caught Loren around the waist and kissed her before rejoining the men.

His lips missed her even as he stood at the table. "Loren just told me she'll make the arrangements with her agent's husband for use of the TV studio that's downtown in the Omni building. She said she'll talk to Dionne about getting the audience. Dionne already planned to be here tomorrow. We can set this up to be a huge production and reel this jerk in. Hugh, Dionne will be expecting you tomorrow."

Hugh nodded. "He just replied he'd be at the meeting. He wants to know where." His eyes shined with excitement. "I'll let him know."

Rob gave him the address and was filled with adrenaline. He always felt this way before a takedown, but this was different. This was personal.

Ben hadn't made a plate and was still standing. "Rob, for obvious reasons, you're ghost with Loren. Now that we have the perfect venue, let's get his real publisher out of the way and secure the location here in Atlanta. This sounds like an all-nighter so that everything goes off without a problem. We're going to catch this man, and we have to make sure we do it in such a way that he never sees the outside of a prison again."

Chapter 26

At 2:00 a.m., Rob limped into the bedroom, and nothing looked as good as Loren as she lay asleep on the bed. He undressed and showered and was emptying his pants pockets when he heard her moving.

"Do you work like this all the time?" she asked.

He looked over at the bed and saw two ponytails sticking up from beneath the covers. "When it's important."

"I heard Ice's voice this evening. She didn't even stick her head in to say hello."

"I told her you were naked. She didn't want to invade your privacy."

Loren hadn't yet turned over, and he wondered if she was angry with him for working late. "Baby, I'm sorry. We needed to get the details worked out on the takedown. We appreciated dinner."

"You're welcome. What did you all talk about?"

"It's late. I'll fill you in tomorrow morning."

"No, Rob. I've been sequestered all day."

"Okay." He climbed into bed, wrapped himself around her and told her everything.

"Can your brothers trick Odesi into showing up?"

"They can do anything," Rob told her.

"Where will the audience be? They can't be onstage."

"They'll be offstage and will be seated once he confesses."

"There's so much that can go wrong, Rob."

He held her closer. "Nothing will go wrong. Don't worry."

The only light in the room came from a thick cherry candle she'd left in a candle burner on the dresser. It was really late, and all he'd been thinking about was getting into bed and making love to her. Rob could see how selfish his thinking was now that she was in his arms. She was wide-awake.

His carnal needs had been long neglected, but he couldn't just take all he wanted from her without making sure she was getting all she needed in return.

She wrapped her legs around him and nuzzled his neck with her nose.

Rob enjoyed her playfulness and tickled her foot. "You haven't had anyone to play with all day and you're bored."

She intentionally stuck out her bottom lip and he almost took her right then. "I've gotten used to us being together," Loren said, and stroked his chin.

Rob reached for her foot, moved down and kissed it.

Loren's eyes widened. "What in the bloody hell are you doing?" She sat up and stared at him, before he pulled her legs up and she was on her back again.

"Kissing your foot. You don't like it?"

"It tickles. Nobody's ever done that to me. Rob, get up here." He watched her closely as he kissed her ankle, then her calf and the inside of her knee.

"Not any of those fancy Italians you dated or your husband for a day?"

"Oh, my goodness," she purred when he kissed the bend in her knees. He paid the same attention to the other leg, and she squirmed on the bed the closer he got to her center. Her hands were all over his back and head, and he liked that this was new to her. "Oh, Rob. What are you doing?"

"It feels good, baby. I promise."

Loren stopped moving and her hands balled into tight fists.

Rob placed his hand in hers, and touched her clit with his tongue. Slowly he made love to the essence of her womanhood, loving the softest parts of her. All of her secrets were open and she shared them with him, her moans of pleasure driving his desire higher.

When his lips touched her nether world she moaned and her legs shook. When he touched her with his tongue she sighed, and when he kissed her, she urged him to continue, wanting more of his love until he took her clit between his lips and coaxed her to a soaring climax.

Her body arched off the bed, and he watched her in all her ecstasy, and there was never a more beautiful sight than Loren in full abandon. She reached for him and he denied her again, turning her over on her stomach so she could see herself as he entered her from behind. She cried out, pushing back against him, setting a steady pace.

"More" was all she said, and he obliged until she came again.

Rob gave her what she asked for until he felt as if he was an exploding sheet of glass, and he had to come apart before being put back together again.

Loren arose early the next morning and cooked breakfast, then boxed the cakes before going upstairs and cleaning. She was going to have to return Zoe's house in pristine order and move into an apartment at her complex, although that was the last thing she wanted to do. She really wanted to stay with Rob, but she realized that wasn't a smart decision. They were a new couple, and she didn't want to pressure him into anything. Besides, she needed her own space. She needed to establish her own life again. The idea made her turn up her nose. She just really wanted to start over with what she had. The pictures of her family and her best friend. Loren scrubbed and wiped down everything until her arms burned and her back ached, and at the end of her cleaning spree she was no closer to being happy about her living situation than she was when she started. But happiness wasn't everything. She accepted what she had to do.

In just over an hour she was finished with the bathrooms and had stripped the beds and was taking the linen downstairs to the laundry room when she heard Odesi's voice in the house. She stopped at the top of the stairs and listened.

"Why would I want to meet with you, Hood? Loren needs a real man with a firm hand. She could never be happy with you. It's too bad you're still alive. She and I need to settle some things."

"Odesi, your problems are with me. You put a hit on my life, and I've taken all your money. Call me when you need a bus pass. Or maybe you can catch a ride with one of your lieutenants."

"You bastard!" Odesi exploded over the cellular speakerphone. "You had them all deported. You will pay for this."

"Now it's my turn to laugh. Go to hell. Coffee, sir?" Rob said politely.

"No, thank you, Mr. Hood. This really wasn't necessary. We could have worked something out."

The ambassador was here in the house? Loren rushed down the stairs.

Dropping the laundry, she ran to the kitchen and was a step away from the ambassador when she realized that Rob was holding a gun on him.

Ambassador Tunaotu sat at the table in a gray-and-white pin-striped suit, his white shirt unbuttoned at the collar. The thin man looked worried, but not afraid.

"What the hell is going on, Rob?" she demanded.

"We're catching a rat and we needed rat bait."

Panic hit her in the chest at what Odesi would do if he knew his father was being held captive. He would burn the house down. He'd kill her ten times. "Rob, he'll tell him where to find me," she said, her voice ringing in her ears. "He'll hurt me again. We have to get out of here. How could you do this to me? Why did you bring him here?"

"He doesn't know where he is."

"It doesn't matter. We have to go," she said, her emotions unraveling. "Please, baby." She tugged Rob's arm. "Ambassador," she started. "I'll give you anything."

Rob caught her arm before she could reach his captive. "Darling, stop right now," he said against the side of her face. "Nothing is going to happen to you. Look at me."

Rob caught Loren in his arm, his gun trained on the ambassador, and made his point. "You are safe. Do you hear me?"

She stood against him and finally looked into his eyes. "Yes, I hear you."

"Get dressed to go on TV," he said, kissing her cheek, daring the ambassador to contradict him. "We've got a long day ahead."

His calm became hers, but the ambassador's gaze was still fixed on her. The fear she saw in his eyes worked its way into her bones.

"Loren," the ambassador said, sadness in his eyes. "He needs help. I swear, no more of this gallivanting around the globe. I mean it this time."

She'd heard enough. Loren lifted her shirt and exposed her torso. "You said you meant it this time, too."

He turned his face away in shame. "He was insane! He didn't mean it! Surely you can see why…how…he needs help."

Ben and Zach walked in, and the Trap Team, joined by Ice. They entered the kitchen through the garage. Nobody said a word about Loren's scars. Xan and Mel surrounded Loren.

"It's okay, sweetie," Xan said to Loren, touching her cheek and covering her stomach. "You're safe. You're with us now."

"I heard you say he's going to get help," Zach said, his voice deadly. "You'd better hope that your brand of help gets to him before I do. I'm after your son's life just like he went after my brothers."

Rob looked at Zach, who walked out. "The clock is ticking, everyone. Let's move out quickly. Ladies, help her get dressed. Ice, get Zach and make sure he gets in the car. Hugh is over at the studio with Dionne and the other staff. We've got a lot of people in motion. Trap Team, don't leave her side. Ben, Zoe must stay with Trap Team. Odesi is desperate. Don't give him any opportunities. Everyone move out."

Chapter 27

The heat inside the van was stifling, but Rob wouldn't let them run the air and arouse suspicion. Everyone was in place, including Loren. She and Zoe had been moved into a studio with Xan and Mel, while Ice, who spoke French, had been put in charge of perimeter security and was working that detail with several of the international officers.

Hugh was giving orders inside and everyone was following his lead.

The ambassador's cell phone rang endlessly and he was finally allowed to answer it. "Hello?"

"Where have you been, Father? My accounts are temporarily unavailable. Some glitch with the bank, and I can't get into yours."

Odesi's father shook his head. "Son, I can't talk right now," he said, going off the script Rob had given him.

Rob shook his head and showed the ambassador by a remote live video feed the punishment for his renegade action. His home safe was pillaged for ten thousand dollars. The old biddies would sure make good use of that money.

The man sighed heavily and nodded his acquiescence. "Son, let's talk. I will not give you money this time."

"I've got to take care of some business in Canada immediately," Odesi screamed hysterically. "A hundred thousand should do it for the weekend."

The ambassador looked at Rob and then the video of his safe

in Buckhead, Atlanta, being emptied, ten grand at a time. "Your accounts should be fine in a couple hours. Just be patient, son. I thought you had a meeting with your editor. Isn't she giving you an advance?"

"That's tomorrow. Stop minding my business, Father."

"Fine, Odesi. It's just that she left a message with Memmi that she was arriving today. I thought you were going to meet her early."

"Why didn't you say that earlier? Did she leave a number?"

The ambassador quoted the number Rob had given him.

"Where is she staying?"

"The Omni, downtown."

"Disgusting." Odesi shuddered audibly. "New Yorkers can be so low class. Thanks for nothing, as usual."

"Son," the ambassador said, but Odesi had already hung up.

The ambassador's head fell back, his expression distressed.

"I'd have written him off a long time ago for treating me that way." Rob sent a message to Hugh, who ordered the team out of the ambassador's house.

"You don't know how he's struggled without a mother."

"Our father died when we were sixteen," Ben told him. "*'Honor thy mother and father and thy days will be long.'* If I die today and go to hell, it won't be because I disrespected my parents."

"It's 'cause you broke that commandment about stealing," Rob told him, and Ben gave him a fist pound. "Got that right. Let's go inside and get this over with."

Odesi walked into the black-curtained room, his nose in the air. "Is this the best they could do? A broken-down TV studio and not a proper conference room? The whole thing looks like it's being renovated."

Former cop Natalie Rush was as cool as ever as she adopted

the persona of senior editor Beth Ann English. She knew her role was pivotal in helping the Hoods take down Odesi Tunaotu, and she was going to do her best to be successful.

She stood, trotted over to Odesi and extended her hand. "Odesi? So nice to meet you in person. Unfortunately the hotel is doing major construction because of the conventions coming in a few months. I was offered this makeshift conference room, and I told them this is fine. We only need it for about an hour. It's all about the work," she gushed, charming him.

As a cop, she'd worked several undercover stings, but this was her most important role, as far as Natalie was concerned. She'd overheard the international police, and they wanted to question him about various charges like rape, sodomy and attempted murder. A lot was riding on this interview. Beth Ann lifted her shoulders and pretended to love everything about Odesi, though he personally disgusted her.

She could hear Rob and Hugh in her earpiece. *Make him feel comfortable.* "Your proposal is, well…outstanding."

He eyed the woman oddly. "Over the phone you sounded like a white woman."

Natalie pressed her lips together and smiled. "I think something happened as the plane crossed the Mason-Dixon line. Sinuses. Please sit down." She crossed her ankles, trying to calm her frayed nerves. "My executive editor will be joining us later, Odesi, but let me say, I'm in love. In love with this book proposal." She stretched out the word and he started to grin.

"We have big plans for you. My, my, you're gorgeous. Whew! How do you walk this earth without women passing out in front of you?"

His chest blossomed as he posed and gave her a profile. "They do. I have women, Beth. They're a weakness of mine."

"Tell me, Odesi. That must have angered Loren."

"It did. She wanted me for herself, and I told her I wasn't a one-woman man. I am an international man," he said with a leer.

"I see." Natalie looked around as if she were too modest to watch his antics. She suppressed the gag reflex and remembered all that they'd rehearsed last night. Loren was safe with Rob right now in the booth, and everyone was depending on her to bring this joke of a man down.

"Ask him about what happened in Monaco," Hugh said into her ear.

"Now, Odesi, I am your confidante. You can trust me with anything. As we talk, I will sign over your checks in ten-thousand-dollar increments. That way it stays under the radar of the government and taxes."

He stood and posed. "Beth, I'm going to need more than fifty thousand. I'm going to need a hundred." He seemed to do a few hip thrusts toward her face and she recoiled.

"A hundred? Why?" Slowly she put her hand on her lap.

He observed her movement and rushed to reassure her. "My circumstances have changed. I can't write here in Atlanta. I need to move quickly."

"Well, that's shocking." She put her head down, then looked up innocently. "Does this have to do with Loren? Is she causing you distress? Is she the reason you want to move?"

Beth had dropped her voice to inspire confidentiality. He dropped into his seat, gazing into her eyes.

"She's constantly calling me. I was visiting a friend and saw her with a street thug, Hood. She caused such a scene, I was arrested. Now, what do I have to tell you to earn this?" He held the check in his hand and nearly pocketed it before he realized there was no writing on it.

Rob kissed the back of Loren's hand as they stood in the booth away from the studio. Cameras had been hidden all around the studio where Natalie and Odesi were sitting, but Odesi had no idea. Rob wanted to walk down the hall and strangle the man, but he kept his emotions in check. "Now we play with the mouse."

"What are you doing?" she asked.

"Pushing him off a cliff."

Rob texted:

Your Manhattan apartment was just raided, your furniture removed. BMW, too. Good day, asshole.

Odesi looked to his phone, then angrily slammed his hands onto the table.

Beth jumped. "Bad news?" She picked up the check and made a big deal of folding it and nearly putting it in her bag.

"No! No," he said, looking anxious. "I need to write this book in solitude. Loren's reemergence is disturbing. I'm thinking Canada. Deep in Canada." Odesi licked his lips.

Beth nodded. "Of course. It's important for an editor and author to speak freely. Canada is no problem. In fact, it may be closer for me to get to you. But I need to know some of the facts. The publisher wants me to know what happened. Nothing you say will leave this room. In your proposal, you say she was cutting herself. Tell me about Monaco."

Beth got up and with the tightest A-line skirt on that was allowable by law, walked over to the bar and made him a drink. Setting it before him, she then opened her computer tablet and started typing. "You talk and I'll type."

He drank the orange juice and looked at the glass oddly. "I thought there was something more in there."

"It's ten in the morning."

"So what?" he said harshly.

Beth smiled. "You're so bad, Odesi. We're going to get along great. I'll have some vodka brought up." Beth made a call. "The cutting," she reminded him.

"She'd been cutting herself for days. I tried to stop her and she wouldn't have it. She was violent."

"Loren?" Beth asked, meeting his gaze evenly.

"Loren," he emphasized, "needed constant attention. I found her on the bed and she was unconscious. What a stupid mess she was."

Beth smiled and put on her heavy-rimmed black glasses. "I have some good news. I've got pictures of her injuries, Odesi. They tell an interesting story."

"How'd you get those?" he asked.

"The photographer who took the original photos for the crime scene kept the negatives. The publisher paid a handsome sum for these pictures for your book. Just look them over on the computer and initial that you remember them as they're shown."

He stared at the photos on the computer tablet and initialed. "She was cutting as I said. These on her arms and stomach."

A knock sounded at the door and Beth took her time getting there. "I ordered some food. You initial." She walked over and met Hugh, who had a cart of food.

"There are no marks on her arms," Hugh mouthed.

Beth wheeled in the tray and served Odesi as he stared at the pictures, scribbling his initials lavishly on the screen. "I love this computer. Can I have one?"

Beth giggled. "You're going to have to buy it out of your first advance." She wrote the first check and gave it to him. "See how easy that was?"

He clapped his hands and accepted the cloth napkin on his lap. "Wonderful. What else? I need a lot more of these."

He ate the shrimp cocktail as if he was starving. "Now, Odesi, five doctors state in their reports that Loren couldn't have administered the cuts to her abdomen. Tell me how you remember this happening."

"Beth, are you calling me a liar?"

It was her turn to clap and laugh. "I don't like unemployment, Odesi. My best friend was fired last month for not asking the hard questions. Let's get this out in the open. Tell me about this one and I'll sign over another twenty thousand dollars. Just tell the truth and I'll be fine."

Opening her briefcase, she showed him the pad of checks and his eyes widened. He wanted all of them.

"I want thirty thousand now. Write the checks, Beth."

"He's getting desperate," Rob warned. "Get up on the table. Your foot in the chair."

Beth obeyed and Odesi's attention shifted to her legs, which were now before him. She began writing the checks. "Tell me, Odesi. I can listen while I write." She handed him the first check. "As your editor, we can rework the language in the book. What was she to you?"

"She had been my woman, but she turned into this greedy, attention-stealing bitch. Nobody was booking me anymore, just her. Her lips were so damned big, and she had that exotic Native American/Black thing going for her. Suddenly that was in."

Beth smiled. "Okay, so what happened? You got angry and cut her?" She signed another check and held it out to him. "So what if you did?" She scrolled up on the tablet and pointed.

Rob leaned into the microphone, staring at the close-up of Odesi's face. The greedy bastard had cocktail sauce dripping down his chin as he leered at the checkbook, then at Beth Ann's legs. He probably had no intention of writing the book. He just wanted the money. He'd talk, he just needed incentive. "Ask him, Beth Ann. Say 'What did you do to her?'"

Beth Ann repeated Rob's words verbatim and Odesi leered at her legs then bit the head off a shrimp.

"I cut her. She was so pretty and I wanted to cut her face off, but she fought like a cat, hitting me and kicking. I wanted her guts to spill onto the floor, but there was blood, Beth."

Rob clutched Lakota to him. "Oh, my God," she said. "He confessed. You did it!"

Controlled pandemonium broke out around them and Rob held Lakota through her trembles and her tears.

Dionne rushed into the booth. "Ladies and gentlemen, it's time to get this show on the road."

Loren hugged her agent so hard and the woman accepted her embrace. "Thank you."

"My darling, it's not over yet. Rob, you're needed for the takedown. I've got to get our girl here into a more glamorous top."

"Tell me, Odesi. Was it all over you?" Beth Ann asked.

"Everywhere," he nodded, closing his eyes. "I got her onto the balcony and tried to get her over, but she held on, the bitch."

"Why?" Beth handed him two checks and pointed to the tablet for him to sign. He initialed.

"Because that bitch owed me. She stole my fame and now I'm finally getting my due. She was garbage, completely disposable." He paused. "Can you make that sound good in the book?"

She touched the tablet and had him sign away his last assets.

A knock sounded on the door. "That's my executive editor. Initial here while I sign the rest of these checks."

"What am I signing?" he asked, stacking his checks, counting them.

"Read it, Odesi. I can wait."

"It says I'm giving this statement freely and without coercion."

She smiled at him. "Are you?"

"Yes. So you can make this sound good?" he asked, licking his lips.

Loren turned into Rob and embraced him tightly. "Thank you, Rob."

Xan and Dionne took Loren away so Rob could finish working.

"Beth, get out of there." Rob's order was clear and crisp and Beth slid off the table.

"Wait!" Odesi grabbed her arm.

"Whoa, buddy. What's the matter?"

"No one will ever know what we've talked about?" he asked, worry in his voice.

"Definitely. Excuse me for just a second. Let me get the door."

Beth gathered her computer and walked away.

The curtains that had been acting as walls fell away to reveal an empty television studio. Almost immediately the studio audience began to file in, looking shocked. They'd watched the entire event in the studio next door. Odesi stood up, but was immediately surrounded by armed police officers.

"I'd like to welcome you to a special edition of *Breaking News* with Odesi Tunaotu, the FBI, and special agents from the Monaco Police Department, and the Atlanta Police Department.

"My name is Natalie Rush, not Beth Ann English, and I am an editor for a magazine, not a New York editor. I'd like to welcome in our studio audience. This rather elaborate plan was set into motion because all a woman wanted was her life back after suffering from domestic abuse."

"This is entrapment!" Odesi shouted.

"These are the pictures you all didn't see of Loren Smith."

Still shots were shown of Loren's injuries right after the crime, and there were gasps and shouts from the audience.

"We're not showing these on TV because we don't want to

taint a jury pool. These shots were taken of Loren today. Large photos of her in two-piece bathing suits, shorts and sexy tops with her scars showing. The angles lessened the harshness of the scars and she looked amazing.

"You can't strike real beauty, Odesi," Natalie told him. "Ladies and gentlemen, I give you Loren, also known as Lakota Sky Thunderhawk."

The applause was deafening.

Silhouettes on long silk screens of Loren unfolded from the ceiling and she was supposed to walk through them onto the stage. Backstage, Loren hesitated. "Come with me," she said to Rob, who'd held her hand through the entire ordeal.

He shook his head. "You can do this part alone."

"I don't want to."

"Then let's go," he told her. Rob took her hand and he walked her to the end of the silk screen and kissed her.

Loren didn't glide or strut, she walked onstage, smiled and waved to the room of women who were just like her: survivors. She removed the white cowboy hat and the jacket and accepted the microphone.

"Odesi, you have no more power over me."

The police escorted him and his father out as the audience continued to honor her bravery. "Thank you. It feels good to be back."

The top she wore was shimmery silver and sleeveless and covered her stomach in thin strands. Loren felt tears build, and for a few seconds she couldn't help herself. Everyone who cared for her was present and she basked in their love.

Natalie talked to the audience to give her the opportunity to gain control of her emotions, and Loren was most appreciative.

She hugged Nera and Tullie and the rest of the biddies. They'd been brought by limousine to the show and would go to the center later to have their party. Dionne had done an amazing job of finding women from shelters to come to the show. It was all done at the last minute. The room was packed and there wasn't a dry eye in the house.

Loren finally took the stage again with a dry face and a big smile.

"Tell us about your journey," Natalie said.

"I was a lot of things. Naive being the first. I thought I had to be quiet in the face of abuse and I didn't know better. I hid from my family and friends. My best friend in the world is here, Zoe, and she didn't know. I almost lost my life."

Loren saw Rob sit next to Ben and Zoe, and Lieutenants Heath and Tuggle, whom she'd invited with their wives. "These really wonderful firemen saved me when I didn't want to go out a window." She laughed. "And I still didn't get that I couldn't hide any longer. Then I had to find a place to stay, and my very best friend had left town with her boyfriend and told me to stay at her house."

Loren blew a kiss to Zoe, who was in the front row, tears on her face.

"She neglected to tell me that she'd left her boyfriend's twin in the house, too." She gave the audience a very sly look and they giggled with her.

"Ladies, I gave him the worst time ever! He wasn't allowed to talk to me, look at me or feed me. And then I injured him." She nodded, looking contrite. "I watered the plants and he slipped and fell...in love with me."

She walked around the stage and collected a tissue from the biddies.

Nera stood up. "Loren, tell them his name is Robin Hood."

The audience laughed, and the cheers were deafening.

"Thanks, Nera that's a good idea. His name is Rob Hood. He told me I was beautiful naked."

Loren touched the hands of the ladies in the audience. She

hugged them and let them see her scars. "Scars were on the inside that needed to heal. I didn't know how to let love in, but Rob was patient with my temper and he cooked my favorite meal of hot dogs... Girls, I know. He won me over and he loves the real me, Lakota Sky Thunderhawk."

She started to cry and put her arm down helplessly. "I believe him when he says I'm beautiful. I love him and I want to have his children. I don't know how to ask him to be with me for the rest of his life. Girls, what should I do?"

"Go get him. Go get him!"

Loren was a chair away and Rob stood up, no crutches, and no cane to aid him.

She reached for him as he reached for her, and Loren caught him just as he caught her.

"I've got you. I love you," they said together.

Their mouths fit perfectly, each knowing they'd found the perfect one for the other.

Epilogue

Lakota and Zoe dressed in silence, trying not to worry. There's no way Rob and Ben would miss their wedding day.

"Let me tie your bowtie for you," Zoe said to her best friend. "You're gorgeous."

"Thank you, darling."

"Now, you. I've never seen such glow to you. You're radiant," Lakota said to Zoe, who wore a gorgeous silk dress with tiny rosebuds that dipped down into her cleavage. "Where do you suppose they are?"

"It takes time to do bad men's work," Zoe explained. "Sometimes I want to just beat the mess out of the bad guys. They know Ben is after them. He's not going to let go. I'm calling him again."

"No, you're not." Lakota took Zoe's BlackBerry and they sat down on the sofa in the den at Rob's, where Lakota and Rob had been living for eight months. "We're going to be patient, even if it means we have to wait all night. This is what we signed up for when we fell in love with them."

Zoe embraced her best friend. "You're right. I love him with my full heart. I love everything about Ben. Even the fact that he can't sing worth a dime."

Lakota wrinkled up her nose. "Rob hammers Luther Vandross terribly."

"Honey, whatever happened to Odesi?"

Lakota sat forward. "His father killed him."

"What!" Zoe reared back, shock all over her face.

"Yes. Just recently, I heard. He said he'd brought great disgrace to their country. His father was deported and will stand trial there. He will, more than likely, get off. Apparently he drugged him, then suffocated him."

"Wow. He killed his son."

Lakota shrugged. "Odesi left a lot of victims in a lot of countries. All those people in all those countries are an international nightmare. It doesn't look good on his father or their country. But his reign of terror is finally over. That chapter of my life is over. Now to my adopted grandmothers. Nera, Lettie, Tully, Myrtle and Hester are the beneficiaries of his unwitting generosity. Remember when Odesi was signing things on Natalie's tablet?"

"Yes. What was he signing?"

"His assets away. I thought he gave them ten thousand dollars." She shook her head. "He signed over a million dollars to them. The rest of his money is going to victims' rights groups."

Zoe chuckled. "I'm sure he was furious."

"Too bad. He'd hurt a lot of people."

"Oh, Lakota. What did he do with your furniture?"

"Honey, he burned it. But that's okay. I got the money and I donated the newly built apartment to be a safe house for women who are abused. It all worked out in the end."

"Lakota, you've done such good things with your show and victims' rights. Even turning more attention to crimes against Native Americans. I can't believe they got a confession out of the guy who killed DeLinda."

"Life is finally working again, Zoe. I'm so happy. I never thought I'd say those words again. Now, if Rob will only come on before our baby—" Lakota put her hand over her mouth.

Zoe gently cupped her tummy. "You, too?"

Lakota nodded. "*Me? You?* I was trying to keep it a secret."

"Twin cousins." The women embraced. "I'm so happy for you," they said together, and started giggling.

Zachary walked in. "What's all this hugging, and I'm not getting any of this love?"

The girls sprang apart and hugged him. "Are they here?"

Lakota looked over his shoulder. "How is Rob? Does he need me?"

"They're here and dressed."

He turned around and offered each of them his arm. "Yes, he needs you. Come on. Let me take you to your husbands."

Lakota took Zachary's left arm and Zoe his right, and they exited the back door of the house and walked down the deck to the newly built gazebo. There were only fifty guests present, and Lakota didn't think they'd be too surprised to see her be impulsive when it came to Rob. She broke loose from Zach and started running, tossing her flowers halfway up the cloth aisle. Much to her delight, Rob broke into a delighted laugh and caught her midjump.

He swung her around. "Lakota Sky, do you take me?"

"I do. Rob Hood, do you take me, and our baby?"

He looked shocked for about a second. Then he squeezed her bottom and she giggled aloud. "I do, you wild woman."

The minister watched the kissing couple. "That was easy. Benjamin Hood and Zoe McKnight, do you?"

"I do!" Ben said, gazing at his bride.

"We do, too," Zoe said, and Ben caught on just as quickly as his brother.

Lakota was happy for Ben and Zoe, but focused her attention on her husband.

She kissed Rob and knew that after all she'd been through to bring her to this moment had been worth it.

Rob hadn't put her down yet, and she hadn't let him go, and she knew she never would. His love was old-fashioned, timeless and rich. She appreciated him every day and all the love, joy and happiness that he'd brought to her life.

His lips caressed hers and she heard the music start. She became aware of people dancing around them in their informal wedding and was glad they'd planned this outside ceremony with just their family and friends.

Lakota gazed up into the man's eyes that she would love forever, and she was glad that she had taken a chance and allowed herself to be loved again. Her feet touched the ground only so they could dance.

"My baby?" Rob asked.

She grinned and nodded. "That's right. Probably a little Lakota."

He shook his head. "God help me."

She grabbed his bottom and put her head on his chest. "You love me."

He did the same thing to her in the body-hugging dress. "You better believe I do. And whatever little boy or girl you give me, we're in this forever."

Hugh walked up to Rob with his phone in hand.

"Go away. I'm about to be a father."

Hugh's mouth fell open. "Man, congratulations." He hugged Rob, then Lakota.

Ben and Zoe wandered over. "I guess I'm riding with Zach on this one," Hugh said. "A university president needs security."

"I think you and Zach will be just fine," Ben said, drinking champagne while Lakota and Zoe sipped flutes of orange juice that Zoe had brought with her.

"Lakota, Zoe, you two are gorgeous," he said. "Welcome to the family. I'll send updates," he said, then saw Lakota's eyebrow inch up. "I'll send them after you get back from your honeymoons," he amended, and walked off to find Zach.

"Do you think they'll find someone?" Zoe asked.

"They're Hoods, baby. We always get our woman, or criminal," Ben replied, taking Zoe's glass and drinking from it. "Orange juice. That's right. Take care of my baby," he said tenderly, nuzzling Zoe's cheek.

"Husband," Zoe said, "come dance with me."

"Sounds good," Lakota said to her husband. Their song came on and she stayed in his arms. "I pledge my heart and my soul to you, Robinson Hood. All my love. Forever."

His eyes filled with tears. "I pledge the same to you, Lakota Sky Thunderhawk Hood."

Their lips met tenderly, and Lakota basked in the love of being in her husband's arms.

REQUEST YOUR FREE BOOKS!

2 FREE NOVELS
PLUS 2 **FREE GIFTS!**

KIMANI™
ROMANCE

Love's ultimate destination!

KROM10

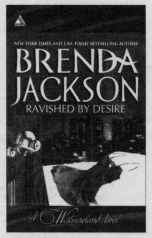